The House of Ibn Kathir

The competition begins...

**BLACKSTONE
HOUSE**

First published in Great Britain in 2013 by
Blackstone House Publications,
PO Box 1091, Harrow, HA1 9HG
www.blackstonehouse.com

Copyright © text S N Jalali 2013
Copyright © cover illustrations and interior
art S N Jalali 2013

A CIP catalogue record of this book is available from
the British Library

ISBN 978 0 9569000 0 5

Printed and bound in Great Britain by CPI
Group (UK) Ltd, Croydon, CR0 4YY

Typeset in Baskerville by Lawrence Mann.co.uk 2013

S N Jalali

The House of Ibn Kathir
The competition begins...

BLACKSTONE HOUSE

www.blackstonehouse.com

Dedicated to my beloved parents,
Sayeeda Banu Khan
and
Syed Mohammed Nazim Jalali

*"O my Lord, have mercy on both of them
as they had nurtured me when small"*

Contents

Chapter One

The Journey to Dar Al Ilm Academy

It is said, 'seek knowledge even as far as China'. It may as well have been for Yusif. He pressed his nose against the window of the car, watching the golden acres of Sussex countryside roll by under the midday sun. The weather was bright, but Yusif was gloomy. He and his parents had been on the motorway for almost four hours. They had left their Birmingham home in the early hours of the morning after the *fajr* prayer, when most other people were tucked up warm and cosy in their beds. But despite the length of their journey so far, for Yusif it seemed as though they were still no closer to their final destination – the Dar Al Ilm Academy for boys, near the coastal town of Hastings.

Yusif could hardly believe what was happening. He had pinched himself more than once to check that he was not dreaming. For tomorrow, he would not be waking up in his own bed at 26 Willowbrook Lane, where he had lived for the last eleven years of his short life. But he would be in a strange bed, in a strange place, miles away from his beloved home and family. Yusif sat gazing out of the window. He thought back to the fateful day when his parents had broken the news to him.

"Boarding school!" he had exclaimed in dismay only a week ago. It was a Monday morning, when his favourite breakfast of scrambled eggs and *halal* sausages was rudely interrupted by the arrival of a curious brown envelope. The letter inside carried the important news of his last minute acceptance into the prestigious school. Dar Al Ilm Academy was no ordinary school, of the type that teaches conventional subjects alone, such as mathematics, English or science. It was also the leading school in the country for Islamic studies and *tajweed* of Qur'an. And it was a *boarding school*!

"But you told me last term that the school had said no!" Yusif protested. "I don't want to go to boarding school Ammi, it's too far away. I will never see you and Abu again!"

He dreaded the thought of being apart from his parents. But he was also thinking of his childhood friends Zayd, Abdullah, William and quite a few others. They had known each other since nursery school, growing up together and spending long summer holidays playing in the park with their bicycles and footballs. Yusif had been looking forward to starting high school with them – a *day school* at that!

Ammi turned to look at him in surprise. She dropped her wooden spoon into a bowl of pancake batter that she had been vigorously beating.

"Of course you will see us again, Yusif,"

she reassured. "There *will* be holidays you know!"

Yusif sniffed his nose, as he made a poor effort to hold back the tears that were welling up in his eyes. Ammi sighed. Ever since she had discovered that a space had become available at the school, she had hoped and prayed that Yusif would win it. Grabbing Yusif, she encircled him in her loving arms and planted a large kiss on his cheek.

"*Subhanallah*, anyone would think you were being fostered off!" she said, smoothing his thick black silky hair away from his forehead so that she could see his eyes. Ammi's hands felt soft across Yusif's brow. She looked directly at him, and smiled. His eyes were dark and larger than average, which gave him an endearing appearance. It was hard for anyone to be upset with him for long.

Suddenly Abu interrupted. He had been sitting across the breakfast table, flicking through the school prospectus, silently observing as the scene unfolded. Noticing that further reassurance was needed, he decided that it was time to offer his opinion on the matter.

"Don't worry son," he assured. "I'm sure you'll make new friends there in no time. Think of all the fun you'll have," he said, holding open the brochure at the 'Outdoor Activities' section. "Look here, they've got archery, horse riding and even a full sized swimming pool – what more could you want?"

Yusif's eyes glanced up curiously, suddenly interested but trying hard to pretend not to be. Archery and horse riding – he liked the sound of that.

It made him think of cowboys and indians. Perhaps it could be fun, he began to concede to himself.

Seeing a hint of change in his son's expression, Abu's tone mellowed a little. He relaxed back into his chair and raised his hand to smooth his well-groomed beard with the backs of his fingers. He always tended to do this when he was thinking. His beard gave him a somewhat distinguished appearance, being neither too long nor too short. Like Yusif, he too had large dark eyes, and despite being in his thirties, there was still a youthful appearance about him.

Taking the opportunity, he looked directly at Yusif and continued with his words of encouragement.

"Imagine Yusif," he said, "what a fantastic opportunity this could be for you. Think of all the wonderful things you could learn. I mean, you always mope around the house after Qur'an class complaining about Ustad Mustafa's new student. What's his name, *aah* – you know the one who is a *hafiz* of Qur'an?" asked Abu, not really expecting an answer.

"Anyway, this is your chance to become a *hafiz* yourself – isn't that what you've always wanted?" he continued, handing the prospectus to Yusif.

Abu was right. There was no denying that memorising the Qur'an in its entirety had become one of his most earnest desires. Completing his first reading of Qur'an over a year ago had felt like a great achievement. But when Abdul Hamid arrived on the scene, things changed somewhat for Yusif.

He was a new student in Ustad Mustafa's class, and although he was only two years older, Abdul

Hamid was a *hafiz* of Qur'an. This had planted the hope in Yusif that he too could be capable of such a great achievement.

Unsure as to whether it is was jealousy that motivated him or inspiration, Yusif slowly began to realise that his ambition could quite possibly be achieved at the Dar Al Ilm Academy.

He pondered on this thought for a moment, shovelling the scrambled eggs around his plate, then mashing them under his fork.

"I know Abu," he sighed flatly, "I do want to learn all that I can. It's just that it's so far away and...what if I hate it there?"

"Then you just come back," assured Abu firmly, "but first you have to give it a chance."

By this time, Ammi had finished folding the pancakes. She brought them to the breakfast table and started drizzling sweet maple syrup over them. Yusif's mouth began to water at the sight of them.

"With plenty of *dua*'s and trust in Allah, I'm sure you'll be fine *inshallah*," Ammi replied in her usual optimistic way. She pushed a plateful of the pancakes towards Yusif, as if it was a bribe. Yusif happily tucked in. 'Perhaps she was right', he thought to himself.

And so it was that the next few days saw Yusif and his family rushing frantically around town, gathering all he could possibly need for his first term at boarding school. Books, uniforms and riding boots were purchased, as directed by the school itinerary.

Of course, Ammi added in all that she could possibly think of, that her little dear 'just couldn't do without'. A new electric toothbrush (to keep the cavities away), a pair of flip-flops (to make *wudu* trips to the bathroom easier) and, despite Yusif's vehement protest, a furry hot water bottle in the shape of a teddy bear (to snuggle up to on cold winter nights). The latter was an item that Yusif had determined to get rid of as soon as he arrived, to avoid the inevitable embarrassment that such a thing would cause.

Time passed quickly and before long, the day of Yusif's departure had arrived.

* * *

Back in the car, Yusif shuffled uncomfortably in his seat. Not the most seasoned of travellers, he was finding it difficult to tolerate the long journey. He glanced impatiently at his watch for what must have been at least the twentieth time.

"Abu, are we going to be there soon?" he pleaded. "How much *longer* do we have?"

"Well, that would be thirty minutes, minus the five minutes from when you last asked me!" replied Abu smiling, as he looked up through the rear-view mirror at Yusif's agonised face. Yusif leaned his head back against the seat and let out a noisy sigh of exasperation.

"Goodness me, you *are* impatient today Yusif," exclaimed Ammi, shaking her head in disapproval. "Remember, Allah loves those who show patience!"

"Well, let's hope that the Academy sorts that out! We do have high hopes for you, you know son," added Abu cheerfully. In fact, Abu only wished that he himself could have had such an opportunity. It was the chance of a lifetime for Yusif, and his father realised what a great blessing this could be for him. It would help him not only in this life, but in the next life too.

"Yes Abu, I understand – I do want to make you proud of me," flushed Yusif guiltily.

Abu glanced again at Yusif through the mirror, with his bushy right eyebrow arching high, as it did whenever something bothered him.

"Proud...? Yusif we *are* proud of you. But son, it is not for your mother's or my sake that we are sending you there! It is for your own good, to help you to become a better person, *inshallah*," corrected Abu.

Yusif silently absorbed his father's words of advice. He knew that his father was indeed a wise and good man, and that both his parents always kept his best interests at heart.

Despite his young age, he was fully aware of how blessed he was to have such a thoughtful and caring family. His father's kindly tone did much to calm his nerves, and helped him to focus on the positives. He tried to reflect upon the adventures that lay ahead of him, until Ammi's voice interrupted his thoughts.

"Yusif darling, don't forget about your night bag. I've packed all the things you will need for tonight," she said. "I can't imagine that the school would expect you to unpack your suitcase straight away. So don't go rummaging around in it for your toothbrush or pyjamas, because you won't find them there!"

She hoped that turning the conversation to a lighter note might help to calm some of Yusif's nerves. Ammi, like many mothers of 11-year-old sons, knew her beloved only child better than he knew himself. She was confident that with his good nature, friendly sense of humour and eagerness to study, he would settle down very quickly at the Academy. No doubt, he would have new friends all around him in no time. She anticipated that his fears of missing home would soon become a distant memory.

Just as she finished her sentence the car slowed its pace. They turned off the main road at the junction for Hastings.

"Look!" exclaimed Abu, pointing into the distance with marked satisfaction. "There's Dar Al Ilm! It seems I was wrong – we're arriving sooner than I expected, and in plenty of time before *dhuhr* prayers, *alhamdulillah!*"

Yusif leaned forward, squinting from the bright sunshine, as he stared out of his window in the direction of his father's finger. Sure enough, etched into the skyline was the impressive grey stone building of Dar Al Ilm Academy. Two imposing towers – one on either side of a large central facade, soared up into the sky. Yusif studied the scene before him. There were woodlands to the far right and he could just about make out the distant glimmer of the sea along the horizon next to them.

He was taken aback by the sheer magnitude of the place. This was to be his home for the next few years!

"It's so big!" exclaimed Yusif, staring in awe, his mouth almost agape. His first impression was a troubled one.

Being such a huge place, he feared that it could well take the rest of his school life to find his way around. No doubt, there would be a maze of corridors and rooms. He could find himself lost for hours on end. Did his parents *really* believe that they would see him again? 'Not likely judging by the size of the place', thought Yusif resentfully. He could go in there, only never to come out again! He began to wonder if Ammi and Abu really knew what they were letting him in for.

But as the car began to draw closer to the school, Yusif saw the grounds in their full splendour. His perturbed mood began to ease.

Dar Al Ilm Academy was indeed an impressive school, built on many acres of land. According to the prospectus, it featured a wide array of facilities, including football and cricket fields, an archery range and even a large set of stables. Reading about it was one thing, but now Yusif was actually beginning to see some of these things for real. He could sense a feeling of anticipation creeping into his heart.

Before long Yusif was imagining himself exploring the extensive grounds, galloping on horseback, and firing arrows towards suspended targets. But despite his growing excitement, he could not entirely shake off the anxiety he felt over this next phase of life he was about to enter.

It was not long before he found himself passing through the school gates and on into the bustling car park, which seemed to be full of families just like his.

Chapter Two

Registration

The car park was choc-a-bloc, filled with the commotion of a hundred families frantically searching for a space to park. Some, having arrived earlier in the morning had already found spaces and were now busy unloading their luggage. Others were eagerly making their way up the large flight of steps that led to the grand entrance of the school. It was a whole twenty minutes before Yusif and his family found themselves standing in the impressive entrance foyer of the school. They were received by a pair of older boys, who had arrived the day before in preparation for the job of welcoming the new boys and returning younger pupils.

Yusif guessed that they were probably sixth formers. They promptly directed him and his parents to the registration desk. Ammi smiled approvingly as she met the two seniors, smartly dressed in the Dar Al Ilm uniform. They sported tidily trimmed beards, and grey blazers embroidered with the school crest. Their shoes were polished so well that she could almost see her reflection in them. She hoped that her own son would one day grow into an impressive, well-mannered young man like these two.

As they moved along a large corridor, Yusif gazed wide-eyed from left to right at the numerous paintings that lined the beautifully carved panelled walls. They depicted grand mosques and scenes from Islamic history. Yusif pondered about the people who had constructed such huge buildings, and what it must have been like to live in those times. His thoughts were suddenly interrupted as they arrived at the 'Orangery', where registration was to take place.

"What an odd name for a room," whispered Ammi to Yusif's father, under her breath. One of their two guides overheard the remark, and promptly offered to give a full explanation about the origin of the name.

The 'Orangery' was in fact a huge conservatory style room decorated with a profusion of plants and flowers. It had been given that name because in the past the room was used to store the orange trees over the winter months to protect them from the frost. It was now used as part of the dining room. But for today's purpose it had been set up as an area for registration and a drop-off point for the new students.

As Yusif and his family entered the great room, they were soon surrounded by pupils, some very young like himself, and others a little older. Some of them looked more like young men than boys, with neat little beards and crisp school uniforms just like Yusif's. He was very proud of his new school attire, which was quite different from what he had worn in the past in his Birmingham school. It consisted of a white *jalabiya* with stiffened collar, a grey blazer with the school logo stitched neatly onto the breast pocket, and finished off with a white *topee* snugly fitting his head.

Yusif sensed an atmosphere of great excitement, as the room buzzed with greetings and joyous reunions.

"*Assalamu alaikum* Muhammad!" shouted a lanky boy from across the hall, "how was the break?"

"Taha!" yelled another, "I thought you said you'd keep in touch – I knew you'd forget!"

Yusif felt a little bewildered at the sight of the new faces. Most of them seemed to know each other so well.

"Look, there's Abdullah!" cried the lanky boy, laughing heartily. "*Subhanallah!* He's fattened up a bit at his mum's over the holidays..."

He gestured wildly towards a rather plump looking pupil, who barely fitted into his school blazer.

"Over here Abdullah! *Assalamu alaikum ya habib*, what have you been eating for breakfast over the hols – parathas, chips, or maybe both?"

An explosion of laughter followed, which seemed to resound around the room. Yusif's lips had curled up into a reluctant smile as he listened to the friendly banter that was taking place.

Despite the merriment, Yusif was suddenly seized by a disturbing thought. He shifted his attention from the group of friends and looked down at his own uniform, as though seeing it for the first time. He became conscious of a sense of apprehension that was growing somewhere deep within him. His uniform fitted him quite well. But how well would *he* fit into his new surroundings? More importantly, would he be able to make friends?

Sensing his uncertainty, Ammi slipped her hands into his.

"You look very smart you know, my darling – just like the other boys," she said in a reassuring voice. "I have to admit, I do love the school uniform."

"Ammi..." asked Yusif tentatively, his eyes fixed on his mother's face, "are you going to be leaving straight away after registration?" He began to feel very lonely, despite the crowds that were now bustling around him.

"We have to pray *dhuhr* first," replied Ammi, "but after that, we must go, I'm afraid. It's the school's request." She smiled at her only child, and patted him affectionately on the head. "But don't worry, we'll make sure you're not left alone when we do."

After some ten minutes of having searched through the rows of registration tables, and being misdirected – twice, Yusif and his parents finally arrived at the right place.

"*Alhamdulillah*, here we are, this is the one...I think," whispered Abu, as he stopped in front of a long white table. It was occupied by an old man. His head was bent downwards, busily scribbling on some sheets of paper before him. Yusif felt his father's arm slip around his shoulders, gently ushering him forwards.

"*Assalamu alaikum* Ustad," said Abu, clearing his throat to attract the attention of the distinguished looking teacher. "My name is Abdur-Raheem, and this my son Yusif Abdur-Raheem."

A pair of hazel eyes glanced up over the antique looking spectacles that nestled neatly on the old man's short straight nose. Yusif studied the new face and could not help but feel an instant warmth towards him. He seemed kind, and his greeting was both polite and welcoming.

"*Wa alaikum assalam wa rahmatullahi, wa barakatuhu* to you all! You are most, most welcome," replied the old man in a distinctly Arabic accent.

"Yusif is joining here in year seven," said Abu very proudly. "This is his first time at the Academy."

"Well young Yusif," said the old man, looking at the rather nervous boy standing before him. "I am sure it will be a great pleasure to look after you. I have a feeling you will settle here with us in no time, *inshallah*." He extended a chubby hand out towards Yusif's, and grasped it with a grip that was so firm, Yusif feared that his knuckles would crack.

"I am Ustad Ibrahim Al Majd," said the teacher, pausing as he scanned the register that lay open on the table. "*Nam* – yes, here you are, Yusif Abdur-Raheem, year seven."

Ustad Ibrahim, was wearing a spotless white *jalabiya* with a crisp grey outer robe. Despite his somewhat surprisingly short stature of five foot and one inch, the learned looking man had a remarkable air of dignified authority about him.

He smiled at Abu and turned his head, upon which he wore a great white turban, to look thoughtfully down at Yusif. Ustad Ibrahim had noticed how closely Yusif was standing to his parents, still tightly holding

his mother's hand.

"Please excuse me one second," continued Ustad Ibrahim, sensing that Yusif was in need of some reassurance. He looked back at the register and then turned his attention towards the crowded room. By now, it was brimming full with families waiting to register their children.

After a second or two he smiled as he spotted the person he was searching for. He raised his right hand into the air, waving it to and fro.

"Reda! Reda Hussein, come over here please!" he called.

Following the direction of Ustad Ibrahim's gaze, Yusif spotted the figure of a boy of similar age to himself. Reda, the boy in question, turned to bid a quick and cheery farewell to his parents. He then emerged from the crowd and headed briskly in their direction. He was tall, with mousy brown hair, bright eyes, and a stocky build. The young lad was very fast on his feet and within moments had traversed the great room to arrive beside the newcomers.

"Ah Reda, *mashallah* I see you've grown another inch over the summer," chuckled Ustad Ibrahim. "And I daresay you will be towering over me before long, eh?"

Reda acknowledged the observation with a beaming smile, before turning his attention towards Yusif, whom he now noted was clearly a 'new boy'.

"Reda Hussein, this is Yusif Abdur-Raheem," said the teacher. "He's one of our new boys. He will be joining your year – and I trust you will help your young brother to settle in, *inshallah*. If I'm not mistaken I think Yusif has had a long journey. Perhaps you could take him to the food tables for some sandwiches and refreshments, while I sort out his enrolment details with his parents."

Reda stepped forward and politely extended his hand to greet Yusif and his father.

"*Assalamu alaikum* Mr and Mrs Abdur-Raheem, Yusif," he said enthusiastically, his smile widening.

"*Wa alaikum assalam,*" replied the trio in unison, pleasantly surprised at such a warm reception.

"Come on Yusif," said Reda confidently, still smiling. "We'd better hurry, the sixth formers are hungry. I saw a bunch of them heading towards the food court. And when they are hungry, *trust me* – you don't want to get caught in the stampede. They're like a herd of elephants! You wouldn't believe how quickly they can clear out the grub!"

With this, Reda grabbed Yusif by his free arm and pulled him away from his mother's hold. He steered him in the direction of the food counters, which despite the efforts of the senior boys, were still laden with a range of delicious treats. Ammi and Abu watched the departure of their son with a much anticipated relief.

"Isn't Ustad Ibrahim cool?" said Reda full of glee. "I hope I have him as housemaster this year! You know, he is one of the best teachers here and not at all afraid of having a good laugh. Everyone else is either strict, or just too serious for my liking," he complained.

"Housemaster?" inquired Yusif, as the pair snaked through the crowds that Reda had so skilfully negotiated earlier, "I don't understand, what do you mean?"

"Oh, there are four houses at Dar Al Ilm!" replied Reda after a short pause, realising that the concept was new to his companion. "Let me think now, there is Ibn Majah House, Ibn Kathir House, Abu Hanifa House and....erm, ah yes! Ibn Ajeroom House."

"In the upper school, we're each allocated to one house, and each house has a teacher responsible over them. You know, to take care of us. We compete against each other. I'm praying that I'll be in the Ibn Kathir House. Ustad Ibrahim is their housemaster, you see," confided Reda.

"You mean, like school teams?" asked Yusif, intrigued by Reda's description. He was beginning to hope that he too would be in Ibn Kathir House. After all, he figured that nothing could be worse than being stuck with a grumpy old housemaster during his time at school.

"Yes, I suppose so, like school teams," replied Reda, as the boys arrived at the snack table.

"So is this your first time away from home?" inquired Reda, as he picked up a tray and placed it in Yusif's hand. He leaned forward to inspect the array of food on offer.

"Yes, it is," said Yusif, pretending not to be nervous about the prospect. In fact, he would have been more nervous had he not been so distracted by his rumbling stomach and the sight of the food. After all, his last meal had been several hours earlier at breakfast time. And even that he had not been able to finish on account of the anxiety over what lay ahead of him that day.

"Have you been at this school long?" he asked Reda, who by now had piled his tray with a variety of sandwiches and other treats.

"Since I was eight years old," replied Reda, helping himself to a large slice of chocolate cake, steeped with whipped cream.

"Eight!" exclaimed Yusif. "I thought everyone would be new." Yusif sighed to himself. He figured that meant most of the kids would have formed their group of friends already, and might not be interested in making new ones.

Yusif looked across at the table Reda had chosen, right next to some tall arched windows that afforded spectacular views of the school grounds. The Hastings sea shimmered in the far distance. But he was in no mood to appreciate it. Holding a chicken salad sandwich, he took his seat opposite Reda.

Reda looked at his silent companion across the table. His eyes twinkled with a knowing look. He remembered how he himself had felt when he first arrived at Dar Al Ilm.

"But of course year seven is when the school has the highest number of intakes," he said in an attempt to put Yusif at ease. "You see most parents don't send their children away to boarding school when they're eight – unless they happen to be *my* parents. They can't decide whether to live in Britain or Jordan, the way they're coming and going. But that's another story. Nope – that's far too young for most. There were only twenty of us in little school, he continued. "I have to admit though, I've been looking forward to this year, you know. We could do with some fresh new faces. So cheer up, you're not the only new kid on the block!"

Reda smiled broadly. He took a long slurp of pomegranate juice and continued with his advice.

"Besides, don't forget you're in good hands with me *akhi – Bismillah...*" said Reda teasingly, as he helped himself to a generous mouthful of the cake.

Yusif smiled with relief for the first time since his arrival.

"Mind, I'm not saying that there's anything wrong with the old crowd though," continued Reda. "Speaking of which..."

But Reda was unable to finish his sentence. Instead, he burst into a sudden fit of laughter, almost choking on his slice of cake. He was looking over Yusif's shoulder at a new arrival on the scene.

"*Subhanallah*, poor Warsoma! Yusif, turn around – you have *got* to see this!" he spluttered, in between his loud guffaws.

Yusif twisted round in his chair to find himself face to face with the extraordinary sight that was the cause of his newly found friend's fit of glee.

There before him stood a very embarrassed young boy. He was being smothered in the arms of his hysterically tearful mother. At the same time, his three elder brothers surrounded him. One was pinching him firmly on the cheek, another ruffling his hair and yet a third gripping him with a firm headlock in an effort to pull him away from their mother's grasp.

The three siblings were mercilessly teasing Warsoma and his mother, playfully repeating her words.

"My baby boy!" she wailed. "Be good now, eat all your greens! And don't forget to brush your teeth at night. Oh, my little boy, my baby!"

"Poor Warsoma," explained Reda. "Every year is the same. His mum overwhelmed with tears, and his older brothers teasing him awfully. He gets so embarrassed. I suppose I should rescue my brother in distress!" Reda stood up and waved at his friend in need.

"Ya akhi, Warsoma – over here!" yelled Reda at the top of his voice. Warsoma, still struggling in his brother's strangle-hold, turned to look in their direction. His anguished expression gave way to one of relief as soon as he laid eyes on Reda.

Notwithstanding a further prolonged episode of *salams* and *duas* from his mother, Warsoma finally broke free from the clutches of his overzealous family, to join Yusif and Reda. With *topee* askew, and spectacles barely hanging on to the tip of his nose, Warsoma collapsed onto the nearest chair.

Slumping his weary head over his arms, he briefly rested upon the table. He caught his breath before looking up in response to Reda's somewhat noisy laughter.

"Go on, laugh all you want!" Warsoma retorted, before sliding his spectacles back up his nose. He looked frantically around in an effort to assess this year's damage to his credibility.

"Do you suppose anyone noticed?" he asked in a whisper.

"It's not so bad, *ya akhi*," comforted Reda. "This year's farewell wasn't nearly as bad as last year!"

"Really?" asked Warsoma relaxing a little in his chair at these much needed words of comfort.

"I mean at least *this* year your brothers didn't pick you up in their arms and carry you off in a procession to the dorms!" laughed Reda.

Warsoma pulled a pained expression on his face, as he recalled the scene from the year before. He remembered how in the weeks that followed, he had been teased awfully by the boys in the year above – until it got out of control. That was when Reda, who was then even bigger than most of the boys in the year above, decided to step in with some friendly advice about the duties of Muslim brotherhood. *That* and the thought of being clobbered by a younger pupil, had put an end to the teasing in the most definitive way.

"I don't get it," complained Warsoma, "can't they see I'm not a baby? I'm eleven-years-old – and mature, I might add. *Ugh – brothers!*"

Reda frowned, but there was a hint of sympathy in his furrowed brow.

"Here, have some of this – that should cheer you up," he said, pushing his half-eaten plate of chocolate cake towards his beleaguered friend.

"You should be grateful you know, *akhi*," continued Reda. "At least you *have* brothers, *Alhamdulillah*. Some people don't have any siblings. Your brothers were only teasing you because that's their way of showing you they'll miss you, that's all."

Warsoma sighed as he took the plate. The cake, although half eaten by Reda, looked delicious, with chocolate cream and sprinkles laced around the edge. 'Most appetising', he thought to himself.

"I know you're right," he conceded, realising how thankful he should be for the blessings he had received. "*Astaghfirullah*, I should be grateful."

Yusif had sat silently throughout this exchange of words. He thought about his own family, and how he had always wanted someone to play with at home. After all, playing football in the garden is no fun if it is just against a brick wall. Being an only child, he of all people should know how it felt.

"I have no brothers *or* sisters," he said. "I always wanted one – it seemed like all fun to me." Warsoma had been so engrossed in himself since joining the table, that he had not even noticed Yusif's presence until now.

"Oh! Warsoma Ghalib..." interrupted Reda, who was feeling guilty for not introducing his companion, "this is Yusif Abdur-Raheem – he's new here."

Warsoma, suddenly aware of his dishevelled appearance, brushed his fingers through the tight, black, curly ringlets on his head. He straightened his *topee* before extending his hand towards Yusif.

"Well, I guess it is fun...most of the time," confessed Warsoma, now slightly embarrassed at his outburst in front of a stranger.

"I think it's great!" exclaimed Reda. "Warsoma is originally from Somalia," he continued. "And he is one of seven kids. Five of them are boys, so you can be sure of a game of five aside footy, eh *Akhi*?" winked Reda. Yusif gasped in amazement.

"Ugh! I hate football *ya habib*, and you know it!" retorted Warsoma. In fact, the truth of the matter was that his younger sister Maryam was more likely to kick the ball around as the fifth member of the team than he was. His dark eyes sparkled as two curious dimples suddenly appeared on either side of his cheeks. He smiled for the first time since joining their table. He was not the most physically active of boys, and made no great secret of his dislike of all things sporting.

Yusif could not help but laugh at Warsoma's reaction. On the contrary, Yusif was quite a keen footballer. He described how he had been a member of the Birmingham Harriers youth football team. Without fail, he had played with his friends twice a week after school.

"Ah *akhi*," assured Warsoma, "you'll settle in here alright then – you won't be short of a game, isn't that right, Reda?"

Reda leaned forward in his chair with a curious look upon his face. He was quietly hoping that the new boy may well become an asset to the Dar Al Ilm football squad, of which he had incidentally been the captain last year.

"Oh, are you any good then?" he asked, for a moment wondering whether his own position may be put in jeopardy by the newcomer.

"Just OK," confessed Yusif modestly, "nothing

special."

Warsoma laughed heartily, sliding his spectacles up his nose again. He had realised that Reda was becoming a little flustered by the possibility of being outdone on the pitch.

"Reda, you're not checking out the competition already are you?" he teased.

"What me..? *Nah*, I wasn't," replied Reda, shuffling uncomfortably in his seat. His cheeks filled with a crimson blush, betraying his embarrassment at being exposed.

Yusif looked from one to the other, with a puzzled expression on his face. "Why, what do you mean Warsoma?"

"Oh, it's just that Reda's a sports freak who happened to be captain of the football team last year. *And* he would like to keep it that way, too!" explained Warsoma.

"Oh, I get it!" laughed Yusif. "Well actually there's no chance of me taking that cap, so I wouldn't worry," he assured.

"No wait, that's not the point, *akhi*," interrupted Warsoma. Clearing his throat quite loudly, he continued with a solemn yet strangely funny look upon his face.

"None of you truly believes until you love for your brother what you love for yourself! Isn't that right *ya akhi*?" teased Warsoma, winking right back at Reda. Reda now a glorious shade of purple, realised that it was time to get his own back.

"Warsoma!" he called out loudly, "isn't that

your big brother Abdeeq over there? I think I'll call him over. You know, I forgot to give him my *salaams* earlier!" Reda's eyes twinkled mischievously. He raised his arm into the air, all but ready to shout out. Yusif, who was very much amused by the antics of his two companions took pity and tugged on Reda's sleeve. And it was just as well. Poor Warsoma looked almost ready to faint at the thought of another round of grappling with his brothers.

By now, Yusif's parents had finished the registration with Ustad Ibrahim. Having spent the last hour reading documents, filling forms, and finally praying the *dhuhr* prayer, they found themselves in the food court. Looking eagerly around, they were delighted to see their son seated at one of the tables, laughing heartily with two of his fellow Academy boys.

Chapter Three

The Prayer Hall

After a much needed lunch, Yusif's parents were in good spirits. They were pleased with the school and felt encouraged by the return of Yusif's good humour. All that was left for them now was to take their leave. Ammi smothered her young son with a teary kiss. She recited *ayat al-kursi*, and reminded Yusif to do so regularly himself. Then she bade her farewells.

Yusif promised both of his parents that he would call them every night. Abu of course, was reluctant to accept such an optimistic vow.

"Hmm, every night? We'll see *inshallah*!" he said laughing heartily. "I suspect you'll be too busy with your studies to keep that promise. So I won't hold you to it...but a great big hug will do just as well for now, come here you!"

Abu encircled Yusif with his arms in a tight bear hug. "Be good!" he said. "We'll see you very soon *inshallah*!"

With that, Yusif and the boys walked with his parents as far as the Great Hall. From there onwards, they stood looking out through the arched windows of the grand old room.

Yusif watched his parents as they got back into the

car. They drove slowly out of the school grounds and through the black iron gates, eventually disappearing into the distance. It was the first time he had ever been without his parents nearby, and he felt both anxious and excited by the prospect of it. He wondered what his next few days would be like without Ammi dragging him out of bed in the morning, or telling him to brush his teeth, or calling him down to breakfast. Only time would tell.

"My parents said I had to go straight to the prayer hall after registration, is that right?" asked Yusif, as the boys finally moved away from the windows.

"Yes, we assemble at the prayer hall for *asr salah*," confirmed Warsoma, as he pulled out a folded sheet of paper from the pocket of his *jalabiya*. "I have the time-table here – see!" Warsoma handed Yusif the paper as he began to explain the schedule.

"After that we will meet the headmaster, Sheikh Ibrahim, all the teachers, the rest of the school and – "

But before Warsoma could finish his sentence, Reda suddenly snatched the sheet of paper from Yusif's hand, buzzing with excitement. Reda was desperate to find out which of the four houses he would be in. Having made no secret about the one he aspired to join, he was eager to get to the prayer hall where the results would be announced.

"Ibn Kathir, here we come!" he cried, almost as if willing for it to happen. "C'mon you two, I'll race you to the prayer hall!"

"But I don't know where it is!" exclaimed Yusif looking around in bewilderment. By then, the huge room in which they stood was almost empty. It looked very different compared to how he had seen it earlier in the day when he had first arrived.

"Oh yes, I forgot..." called Reda over his shoulder as he bolted towards the corridor, "follow me!"

Yusif and Warsoma took to their heels, following their ardent companion just a few paces behind. Warsoma was trailing behind, protesting all the way about what may happen to them if they were caught running in the corridors by the senior prefects – especially the dreaded brother Luqman.

But Reda paid no heed. He led the boys back through the canteen. They passed through a set of double doors that opened out into a breathtakingly large courtyard that stood in the centre of the school building.

Yusif marvelled at the beauty of the place. It was amazing! It looked like a scene from an exotic Moroccan painting. Beautiful mosaic tiles of rich colours embellished the walls. The flooring, paved with white flagstones, dazzled under the glow of the afternoon sun. The sound of rippling water resonated gently around the courtyard, as it flowed from an elegant fountain that stood at the centre of the square.

However, there was no opportunity at that moment for Yusif to stop and further examine the scene. Reda was already on the other side of the courtyard, ready to hurl himself through another set of double doors. As he ran, Yusif did all he could to breathe in the fragrant air of the courtyard. The smell was a mixture of exotic plants and the smoky scent of incense that was burning in one of the far corners of the place.

The boys sped through yet another corridor and passed a few small classrooms that jutted off on either side. Finally, they arrived at the prayer hall. Yusif was stunned by the grandeur of the place.

He stood transfixed under a huge dome, decorated with intricate Islamic calligraphy. At the centre of the dome was the name of Allah, and that of the beloved Prophet Muhammad, peace and blessings be upon him. Around them in slightly smaller script, but nonetheless equally impressive calligraphy were the names of the four righteous Caliphs – Abu Bakr, Umar, Uthman and Ali.

An ornate chandelier hung suspended from the centre of the dome, sparkling as the bright sunlight reflected from its crystals. A large stained glass window, decorated with geometric patterns, in keeping with Islamic traditions, adorned the far wall. At the front of the room stood a tall, dark, wood-carved *minbar*, with stairs leading up to the platform where the Imam of the Friday *jumah* prayer would stand. These ornate features added to the sense of awe Yusif felt as he looked around the hall.

By then, quite a large number of pupils had congregated. Unlike Yusif, most of them were not new to the prayer hall, and evidently lacked the wonderment that had struck the new boy. After finding a suitable spot, he sat down on the floor. There in front of him, Yusif saw a crumpled copy of the enrolment letter. Recognising the contents from Warsoma's copy, he picked it up, smoothed it out and read :

After registration, all students are expected to promptly make their way to the prayer hall for asr salah, which will be offered in congregation. Thereafter, you will be assigned to your respective houses and will meet your new housemasters. The headmaster will then address you. Please be punctual.

'This is it, there is no turning back now', thought Yusif to himself. He looked around at his fellow Dar Al Ilm pupils.

All the boys sat cross-legged on the emerald green carpeted floor. Some looked anxiously to the front of the hall, eager to make a good impression upon their teachers. Others whispered amongst themselves, speculating about what excitement the forthcoming term would bring.

At the side of the *minbar* in front of them sat a distinguished row of teachers, thoughtfully surveying their prospective pupils. Yusif studied them curiously, looking from one to the next. He had never seen such a large number of scholarly looking people in one gathering. His close scrutiny of the staff was interrupted by a sudden tug at his sleeve. It was Warsoma. He was crouched behind him, gasping for breath. His face was moist with beads of sweat from their vigorous run. He leaned forward, his voice barely above a whisper.

"Look – that's Abdul Kadir. He's the head boy," said Warsoma, gesturing towards a small group of older pupils behind them. "They're going to pray *dhuhr salah*. He's the one leading, see!"

Yusif glanced in the direction of Warsoma's slim pointed finger, and watched the group lining up in straight, regimental rows. At the head of them stood the figure of a tall, slim, young man, who despite his size, was clearly attired in the distinctive Dar Al Ilm uniform.

"I need to pray *dhuhr* – have you prayed?" whispered Warsoma.

"No – I haven't," confessed Yusif, as he realised the fact. In all the commotion since his arrival, the thought of the *salah* had completely slipped his mind!

"Come on – we'll join them. Where's Reda?" said Warsoma, as he paused to look around, suddenly aware of the beads of sweat sliding down his lenses. He took off his spectacles and wiped the lenses clean before putting them back on his face.

"I'm right here *akhi*," said Reda who had crept up quietly next to them. "You guys took your time getting here!"

At this, Warsoma sneered with dissatisfaction. 'What a cheek', he thought to himself, recalling the aching stitch he had developed at the side of his stomach from the fast pace of their run. Not to mention a bump to the head as he scampered behind a pillar in an effort to avoid the shrewd eyes of brother Luqman, who had emerged from the ablution room, dripping with water.

"What! Took our time?" exploded Warsoma. "Maybe it's because we don't have stilts for legs – like you! Besides, I hope you realise we were inches away from being caught by Luqman – and spending the rest of the term in detention at break, or even worse – *litter duty!*"

Reda grinned with an all too familiar look of mischief on his face. It was a look that Yusif was coming to recognise. But before Warsoma could respond further to Reda's provocations, Yusif broke in.

"C'mon Reda, we're going to join the *jama'ah* over there. Quick, it's about to start!"

With the argument thus successfully diverted, they hurried forward to join the *jama'ah*, which had assembled behind Abdul Kadir.

Abdul Kadir's voice was as clear as crystal. His pronunciation of the *takbir* had an air of eloquence and strength. Although the *dhuhr salah* was a silent one, Yusif knew that the head boy's recitation of Qur'an must be splendid as well. He had never participated in a congregational prayer *at school* before in his life, and this was certainly a new experience for him. As the prayer drew to a close, Abdul Kadir offered the *tasleem*, turning his head from right to left, signifying the end of the prayer.

At this point, Yusif caught his first glimpse of the head boy's face. He was a kind, intelligent looking young man, and Yusif felt an instant liking towards him. After a few moments of contemplation, Abdul Kadir made a brief *dua* and prayed a further two units of *sunnah* prayer. Once he had finished, he slowly changed from his position and turned to face the boys who had followed him.

It was hard to believe that the figure who sat before Yusif was but seventeen-years-old. His hair was thick and cropped short. Like most of the sixth formers, he wore a very neat beard that was jet black, which made his already slim face appear longer. But at that moment, what struck Yusif the most was not so much his physical appearance; rather it was the air of confidence that surrounded him, as he quietly sat contemplating in *dhikr*.

Yusif was so absorbed in his scrutiny, that he did not realise how curiously he seemed to be staring at Abdul Kadir. That was, until the brother in question caught his sight and smiled with a nod. Yusif flushed with embarrassment, but soon found his composure and returned the smile.

"Abdul Kadir's family is originally from Turkey," whispered Warsoma, as he observed the exchange between Yusif and the head boy. "He's been here at Dar Al Ilm for more than six years."

"Can you imagine, they say he has a photographic memory!" continued Warsoma, evidently very much in awe of the brother. "He had the highest score in the county for Maths. He is also a *hafiz* of Qur'an. Did you know, it only took him two months to memorise *surah Baqarah*?"

Yusif was very much intrigued, particularly as it was his own ambition to one day memorise the Qur'an.

"Why, how long does it normally take to memorise *surah Baqarah*?" he asked.

"Look at it this way, *akhi*," replied Warsoma, "I've been here two years and all I've memorised is the last thirtieth part of the Qur'an, *surah Yasin,* and I'm only a quarter of the way through *surah Baqarah*!"

He gave a muffled moan, throwing his hands up in the air in exasperation as he did so.

"A quarter of the way – are you nuts? That's amazing!" gasped Yusif, lifting his eyebrows despite Warsoma's apparent cynicism. "I've only managed to memorise the last thirtieth part of the Qur'an and that's taken me all my life so far!"

Before Yusif could continue, he felt a sudden jab at his side. Rubbing his arm, Yusif turned to look at the offender who had elbowed him. It was Reda. He had just shuffled forward after the *salah*, replacing a year nine pupil who had been next to Yusif during the prayer. Reda had not managed to squeeze into the same row when they had joined the prayers. Instead, he had joined a new line that had begun to form behind his two friends. Yusif and Warsoma had been so absorbed in their discussion that they had not noticed that their companion had discreetly joined them.

"Ouch! What was that for?" cried Yusif. Reda mumbled a half-hearted apology, but was looking clearly distracted. Curiously, Yusif followed Reda's startled gaze. 'Whatever could have upset Reda like that', thought Yusif? He was soon to find out!

"*Akhi*, we have to leave quick! Brother Luqman is heading this way – see!" whispered Reda urgently, as he pointed towards the stern figure of Luqman. And sure enough, having just left the front row of the *jama'ah* he was heading straight for them!

Luqman Bensalem, an Algerian in origin, had been appointed senior prefect after having graduated into year twelve. With this position, he had earned the right to issue penalties to any juniors whom he saw misbehaving. He was the kind of brother who took no nonsense, and had gained a fearful reputation amongst the younger pupils for it. Taking his new role rather seriously, Luqman had become a regular sight, to be seen roaming the corridors of Dar Al Ilm. Over the preceding months, he had broken the school record for issuing the most detentions.

Although not the most popular member of the school, Luqman felt more than adequately compensated by the increase in his status. With his position of senior prefect, he was now entitled to have a silver badge in place of the previous green one, which he proudly wore on the lapel of his ever smart grey blazer. This combined with his tall stature, made him a formidable sight as he made his regular patrols during break times and otherwise.

As Yusif observed him, he reminded him of an eagle about to swoop upon his prey. Indeed on closer inspection, he *did* in fact look like an eagle, with his long beaky nose, dark brown eyes and bald head. Of course, Luqman was not naturally bald – he had just returned from a trip to Makkah with his family over the summer holidays. His shaved head signified the end of the rites performed during *Umrah*.

"I can't believe it – the first day is not even over and you've already landed us in trouble!" moaned Warsoma. He folded his arms across his chest, as a gesture that he would remain firmly seated, ignoring Reda's suggestion to flee. Warsoma had come to the sensible conclusion that to run now would be folly, especially now that Luqman had clearly realised that the boys had seen him.

"Ssh! Will you let me think!" said Reda, burying his head in his hands. Yusif looked helplessly from Reda's agitated posture to Warsoma's angry one, before glancing back at Luqman to see his progress through the crowd of pupils. Trouble – and on the first day! What on earth would his parents make of this, thought Yusif? After all he had never been in trouble before at school – he had always been a model pupil in the past. But as the boys sat anxiously contemplating their fate, the unforeseeable occurred!

A sudden gasp of relief emerged from all three boys in unison, as the head boy Abdul Kadir stopped Luqman dead in his tracks. Warsoma adjusted the spectacles over his nose, wondering if his eyes were deceiving him. But they were not – for sure enough Luqman had been completely side-tracked by an impromptu conversation with Abdul Kadir.

Reda quickly jumped to his feet, taking full advantage of the opportunity.

"C'mon you two, here's our chance to escape," he whispered. "Nobody would expect us to wait for him – who knows how long they will talk for!"

Yusif and Warsoma likewise rose to their feet, clearly showing no signs of opposition. They hurriedly made their way towards a group of pupils seated under a banner that read 'Year Seven'.

Reda once again led the way. As the boys traversed the prayer room, Yusif glanced back over his shoulder one last time. But what he saw almost made him stumble in disbelief. Luqman by now had his back to them, and was completely oblivious to their great escape.

Abdul Kadir was looking over Luqman's shoulder as they talked. He stood smiling, his eyes glittering in amusement, but not because of anything Luqman had to say. That would have been asking for the impossible! In fact, Abdul Kadir privately considered Luqman to be a bit tedious and egotistical at times. So when occasions arose necessitating his company, Abdul Kadir bore him with patience. To his credit, this was one of his greatest strengths of character.

To ascertain what was afoot, he had only to look from the three anxious faces of Yusif, Reda and Warsoma to that of Luqman's, who was taking long, confident strides in their direction. He had realised that the three youngsters were in for some trouble. Abdul Kadir did not quite approve of Luqman's harsh sense of discipline. He quickly rose to intervene and prevent the three young boys from having a bad start to their year. He had also made a mental note to speak to the headmaster Sheikh Ansari about the matter.

Yusif smiled with relief. As he sneaked away with his two friends, he noticed Abdul Kadir wink in his direction. Had Abdul Kadir just helped them get away, wondered Yusif? How strange...but there was no time to think further. Within moments, Yusif found himself squeezing between the seated boys towards a row that was not yet full. He dropped to the floor, and then shuffled across the soft green *sajadah* which carpeted the prayer hall, making space for Reda and Warsoma.

He sat crossed leg on the floor and faced forward to inspect the row of teachers who sat at the front of the room. All were immaculately dressed. Some had crisp white *jalabiyas*, coats and turbans whilst others wore the more casual attire of prayer cap, tunic and trousers.

One teacher stood out in particular from the rest. Yusif imagined him to be something like a character from the pages of an Arabian Nights' tale. His turban was green and quite large, having been folded around the head several times over. It was a wonder his small head had not given way under the weight of it, he mused. The teacher had a long black beard and thin moustache, and was attired in a dark *jalabiya* to match. There was something mysterious about him, as he sat with his beady eyes looking from face to face at the assembled pupils.

"That's Ustad Zakariya Othman – he's the science teacher," warned Warsoma. "Be careful, he's strict. Get on the wrong side of him and you'll have essays to keep you going till half term!"

"And the quiet one on the end with the prayer beads is Sheikh Ahmad Ghifari," he continued. "He teaches Islamic history – one of my favourite subjects. He's very calm and patient – you're not likely to get into any trouble with him!" approved Warsoma.

"Oh, and the one who's sneezing over there, that's Ustad Nuh Ali, the maths teacher! He has allergies, you know, and sneezes at almost everything. Dust, chalk, and even Reda's awful choice of *itr* – I mean perfume oil!" laughed Warsoma.

"Eh? Very funny!" interjected Reda, as he caught Warsoma's last remark. "I'll have you know that was the finest *itr* you'll find in Jordan! Look, I've got another one," protested Reda as he pulled out a small glass bottle from the inside pocket of his blazer. "It's called Waters of the Nile."

Quickly removing the lid, he held it out under the boys' noses, whilst inhaling the scent most appreciatively.

"*Aaah!* See, I don't know why he had a sneezing fit last term! But it couldn't have been because of me," laughed Reda. Warsoma, however, begged to differ, his nose wrinkling in disgust from the sheer potency of the scent.

"Yuk! Reda it's disgusting – so sickly sweet and far too strong!" he said, covering his nose tightly with his hand.

"Maybe you should throw it back into the Nile, where it belongs!" Yusif also drew back, slightly overcome by the smell.

"It's no use *ya akhi*," laughed Warsoma. "Reda has no sense of smell left. He can't tell the difference between good and bad let alone weak or strong!" Pinching his nose tightly, he turned to Reda and begged him to put away his offensive scent before they all passed out!

"Maybe you should just stick to the *sunnah* of the Prophet and use musk!" he added.

Reda chuckled, waving the bottle one last time in

front of their faces before carefully returning it to the safety of his inside pocket.

After he had recovered from the nasal assault, with his sense of smell now returning to normal function, Yusif turned his attention back to the row of teachers.

"And who's that teacher next to Ustad Nuh?" he enquired. "Let me guess – a teacher in sporty *jalabiya* and white socks – he must teach PE right?" suggested Yusif. He observed the athletic looking man, who clearly appeared to be one of the youngest teachers.

"Yep, that's Ustad Hamza al-Buruni, and he's my favourite!" exclaimed Reda.

"I thought Ustad Ibrahim was your favourite!" teased Yusif remembering their earlier conversation in the Orangery.

"Well, okay, two of my favourites, I guess," admitted Reda sheepishly.

"And speaking of Ustad Ibrahim, where is he, I can't see him?" asked Yusif, craning his neck in search of the familiar face.

But before anyone could speak further, the *adhan* for *Asr* prayer echoed round the prayer hall, sending everyone into a momentary silence. To the left of the *minbar*, a door that Yusif had not noticed before suddenly swung open. Two figures emerged. The first to walk through was Ustad Ibrahim, followed by another whom Yusif recognised from the school prospectus as being the headmaster, Sheikh Muhammad Harun Ansari.

Dressed in crisp white robes he appeared to almost float across the room as he took his place at the head of the congregation to lead the *asr* prayer. Whilst not particularly tall, there was a definite presence about Sheikh Ansari.

He was the type of person for whom it would be very difficult to go unnoticed, wherever he was. His hair was silvery white, as was the beard on his face. These features only added to the strong air of wisdom that exuded from him.

After the *adhan*, the boys assembled for prayer. Sheikh Ansari paused for a moment at the front to inspect the whole school. The entire *jama'ah* stood in neat, ordered lines. The first row was formed of the teachers and sixth formers, followed by the pupils, in descending order of age – from year eleven, right through to year seven at the back. Satisfied with his inspection, Sheikh Ansari turned his attention back to the first row, where the sixth formers stood with the teachers. He nodded his head towards one of the sixth formers who promptly took a step forward.

Yusif instantly recognised Abdul Kadir, who cleared his throat and called the *iqamah* in a loud and melodic voice.

"It's a privilege only granted to the head boy," whispered Warsoma excitedly. "They can perform the *iqamah* before a prayer, if requested by the head! He can even lead the school in the prayer itself, if the teachers are unavailable."

"I'd love to be the head boy when I get to sixth form, *inshallah*!" confessed Warsoma.

Yusif thought to himself how great it would be to be able to perform such a role, but instantly dismissed the idea, imagining that the role was far beyond his capability.

Soon, Abdul Kadir had finished the *iqamah*. He slipped back into his row and joined his fellow classmates. A deep silence descended upon the room as Sheikh Ansari raised his hands to his ear lobes. He called the *takbir* that signified the start of the *asr* prayer.

Chapter Four

The House of Ibn Kathir

"On behalf of myself and all of the staff, *Assalaamu alaikum wa rahmatullahi wa barakatuhu*. Welcome to you all, old and new boys of Dar Al Ilm Academy."

Thus was the headmaster's greeting, as Sheikh Harun Ansari addressed the Academy boys before him. A chorus of '*Wa alaikum assalam*', resounded from the pupils who were still seated in their rows. The Sheikh continued with his opening speech.

"Firstly, as always, we begin with a reminder about the importance of the use of time..." Yusif leaned forward to listen, his attention fully drawn by the warmth and sincerity of the Sheikh's voice.

"We are here on this earth for one purpose only. To worship our creator Allah, all praise is to Him. We have been charged to live by His guidance, as it was revealed to our blessed Prophet Muhammad, may peace be upon him. Through this, we must strive to better ourselves as human beings."

The Sheikh paused before reciting some verses of the Qur'an, which flowed effortlessly from his lips.

"He's a *hafiz* of Qur'an, and a learned scholar,"

whispered Warsoma in Yusif's ear, as they sat side by side. Yusif's lips twitched into a brief smile, not wishing to be too distracted from the sermon. From such a great Sheikh, of course, Yusif had not expected anything less!

The Sheikh's reminder to the school was clear and simple. It was essential for the boys to make the most of their time at the Academy. The school would provide the tools for their development. It would offer knowledge both for worldly goals, as well as for the life in the hereafter.

But it was down to each pupil himself to buckle down and realise these opportunities. The words reminded Yusif of what he had read in the school prospectus in the weeks leading up to his arrival. Now he was here for real. *This was it.* Yusif sensed a glow inside him as he listened, a mixture of excitement and trepidation.

"Time is a trust from God. Whether or not you pass your exams with flying colours, is decreed by the will of Allah. But it is your efforts made here – and in your whole lives, that count. And no doubt, your hard work will be appreciated by both your teachers and peers around you. But never forget that your actions will be judged by Allah in the hereafter."

"So, for those of you who failed to work last year, and you know who you are..." Sheikh Ansari paused to look knowingly around the room. The few guilty shuffled uncomfortably in their seated positions, whilst the rest of the school could be heard stifling their laughter.

"...the opportunity for a 'second chance' lies before you," continued the Sheikh.

Inspired by the speech, Yusif found himself warming towards the Academy. The thought of spending the next three terms here was looking more and more appealing.

"Secondly, some good news," continued Sheikh Ansari. "You will all be happy to hear that the Dar Al Ilm Academy for boys dominated the league tables once again this year, scoring excellent results in the end-of-year exams."

This announcement heralded a loud cheer from the Academy boys. Sheikh Ansari smiled broadly. Waving his arms downwards, hushed the boys back into a quiet murmur.

"However..." he continued, "I must also add that our sister school Dar Al Ilm Academy for girls, out-performed you in the leagues!" Yusif smiled at this piece of news, which provoked great moans from around the hall of assembled pupils.

"Nevertheless, we congratulate them, and all of you! And we hope you will take a leaf out of your sisters' book this year and work even harder – for your houses and the Academy, *inshallah*."

Sheikh Ansari continued his speech. "Speaking of houses, I think it's time we reveal to the year seven pupils which houses they will be joining."

Reda, who had been eagerly anticipating this news for some time, leaned forward and listened intently. He could feel his heart begin to step up its pace, and a tingle ran down the back of his neck. Yusif, who could sense his companion's excitement, shuffled in his position.

"For those of you who are not aware," explained Sheikh Ansari, "there are four houses in the school – each of which is named after a prominent scholar from our Islamic heritage. You will each be allocated to one of the houses, and every year the houses compete with each other."

To Reda's frustration, the next few minutes were spent outlining the rules. As Reda had been in the school for some time, he was already well acquainted with them, and found the delay almost unbearable. Yusif listened thoughtfully, very much intrigued by the concept.

There had been no such houses at his last school, so he had not quite understood what they were. Even when Reda had tried to describe them earlier when the two had first met, Yusif had been left very much baffled by the whole subject. His fascination increased with Sheikh Ansari's descriptions.

Yusif learned that the houses and their members would undertake individual tasks, group projects, and sports activities. All of these provided opportunities for pupils to raise points for their allocated houses, which were in direct competition with each other. Each house would work hard to gain the greatest number of points. The points would then be tallied at the end of the year and compared, to establish which had attained the highest score.

The winning house would receive the esteemed Dar Al Ilm Trophy. In addition, the year captain for the following year would be chosen from the winning house by votes from the boys, housemasters and the headmaster himself.

The pupils of year seven held their breaths. The moment had come for each boy to know which house he would occupy for the duration of his time at the Academy. It would also reveal who was to be their housemaster. After a moment's pause, which seemed to Reda and Yusif like an eternity, Sheikh Ansari made the announcement.

"The first is the House of Ibn Majah," he said. "It is named after the famous *hadeeth* scholar *Abu Abdallah Muhammad ibn Yazid ibn Majah al-Rabi al-Qazwini* otherwise known as Ibn Majah. The housemaster will be Ustad Zakariya Othman." He signalled to Ustad Othman, who stood up and promptly stepped forward to stand beside the Sheikh.

"The second – the House of Ibn Kathir, is named after the famous scholar of *Tafseer, Imad Ad-Din Ismail ibn Umar ibn Kathir Al-Quraishi Al-Busrawi* otherwise known as Imam Ibn Kathir. The master over this house will be Ustad Ibrahim Al-Majd." Sheikh Ibrahim duly stepped forward to take his place beside Ustad Othman.

"The third is the House of Abu Hanifa, who is known by many as 'The Great Imam'. He was a scholar of *fiqh, Nu'man ibn Thabit ibn Zuta bin Mahan,* otherwise known as Imam Abu Hanifa. And the housemaster will be Ustad Saif Uddin O'Malley."

Yusif looked to the line of teachers sitting behind the headmaster, but saw no movement. Warsoma had not mentioned that particular name earlier. Yusif stared at the teachers' faces, recalling their names one by one, wondering to himself which one this might be.

Sheikh Ansari himself turned round to look at the teachers, also slightly surprised that no one had stepped forward.

"Oh! It would appear that we are missing Ustad O'Malley for the moment. In that case, let us move on to the next house." He continued with the proceedings.

"Finally, the house of Ibn Ajeroom, which is named after the respected scholar and Arabic grammarian, *Abu 'Abdillah Muhammad ibn Muhammad ibn Daawud as-Sanhaajee*, otherwise known as Ibn Ajeroom," announced Sheikh Ansari as the last of the housemasters stepped forward to join the line. "The master presiding over this house is Ustad Nuh Ali."

Just then, Ustad Ali's introduction was interrupted as the entrance door of the hall suddenly burst open. A young man walked hurriedly in, wiping beads of perspiration from his face with his handkerchief. He apologised profusely for his tardiness, explaining how his train from Charing Cross station had been delayed, and that he was lucky to have made it there at all.

"That's Ustad O'Malley," whispered Warsoma. "He's a revert from Ireland. He teaches English language and literature." Ustad O'Malley looked very tired and flustered, with his cheeks flushing bright red. Travelling all the way from Ireland first thing in the morning had clearly taken its toll on him. Sheikh Ansari allowed a moment for Ustad O'Malley to compose himself, who then took his place beside the other housemasters to complete the line.

With the houses and their masters thus formally introduced, it was at last time to reveal their student members. Sheikh Ansari stepped aside, leaving the rest of the proceedings to the various masters.

Ustad Zakariya Othman was the first to speak. He pulled out a sheet of paper from his inside pocket. All eyes were upon him as he slowly unfolded the document. Reda gulped in anticipation. With a slight cough to clear his throat, the Ustad started to call the names of pupils who had been allocated to the House of Ibn Majah.

Yusif felt a sudden panic rise within. Butterflies arose from somewhere deep in the pit of his stomach. What does it *really* mean to be in a house, he wondered to himself. After only just making friends with Reda and Warsoma, was he now to be separated from them? Would they even be in the same classes?

All of these questions ran through his mind in an instant. He wanted to ask his friends, but that could mean missing his name in roll call. There was no choice but to stay silent for the moment.

"Usman Ahmed, Faisal Attia, Sufyan Hamdi ..." one by one the names followed. Until to Yusif's relief, the list drew to an end. There was no mention of any of the three boys' names.

Ustad Zakariya put his list away inside the folds of his *jalabiya* and moved back to his former position. Then, Ustad Ibrahim stepped forward. He paused for a second, peering over his glasses at the nervous faces gazing eagerly back at him. He smiled sympathetically, and began to announce the names.

"For the House of Ibn Kathir, the following pupils will be joining us. Numan Abdul Basset, Yusif Abdur-Raheem..." Yusif's heart leapt as he heard his name. Warsoma and Reda turned and looked nervously in Yusif's direction. While they were happy for Yusif, they were nonetheless, worried as to their own fate. All Yusif could do now was to pray that if not both, then at least one of the two friends who sat beside him would be called.

"...Zulfiqar Ali, Muhammad Diwan, Warsoma Ghalib ..."

Yusif's heart skipped another beat. Warsoma was in '*Alhamdulillah*', thought Yusif, as he gasped with relief. Reda now sat with his chin pushing down on his hands, which were clasped so tightly together that his knuckles had turned white. He whispered under his breath, frantically making *dua* that his name would be called. Yusif and Warsoma exchanged helpless looks. All they could do now was to pray for Reda's name to be called.

"...Harun Gibbs, Amar Hasan, Reda Hussein, Daud Llewellyn-Jones..."

"Yes!" cried Reda, unable to contain his joy. His voice echoed around the room, which had until then been quiet, save for the sole voice of Ustad Ibrahim. Curious heads turned to look at Reda, who was by then flushing red with embarrassment at his outburst. A few of the older boys grinned.

It was an outburst that also did not go unnoticed by

the staff members. Realising that he had inadvertently made himself the centre of attention, Reda began to look very meek, as he noticed Sheikh Ansari raise his eyebrow in disapproval. Ustad Ibrahim himself shook his head at first, peering over his glasses as he looked directly towards the offender. In fact, he was very much amused by Reda's flushed face, and could not help but let slip a smile. A gentle murmur arose from the back of the hall.

The booming sound of Sheikh Ansari's staff striking down on the marble floor of the *mihrab* silenced the room in a moment. With order thus restored, Ustad Ibrahim continued calling the names on his list.

"You really know how to lay low on the first day!" whispered Warsoma sarcastically, leaning forward towards Reda.

"Actually, I didn't think anyone would hear me," grinned Reda, his spirits now fully restored.

"*Subhanallah,* those were the longest couple of minutes of my life!" he said. "For an awful second I honestly thought my name wouldn't be called!"

"Me too!" agreed Yusif. But he could comment no further. For Musa Akhtar, who was sitting in front of the boys, turned to look at them – quite annoyed.

"Ssh, will you!" he hissed, bringing his fingers to his lips in a gesture of silence. "I'm trying to hear the list for the House of Abu Hanifa. So if you don't mind – zip it! "

And so the next few minutes passed with the three friends sitting in silence. They happily listened to the proceedings, comfortable in the knowledge that their hopes had been satisfied. With the roll call finally complete, Sheikh Ansari stepped forward once more to address the year seven pupils, with a final word of advice and encouragement for the new academic year.

"Let the competition for good deeds begin!"

With that, the housemasters rounded up their year seven pupils. The boys were formed into four lines, one for each house. Before long, the pupils of the House of Ibn Kathir – Reda, Warsoma and Yusif among them, were marching in orderly fashion out of the prayer hall. They proceeded into the courtyard, with a cheerful Ustad Ibrahim at their head. Their destination was to be the Ibn Kathir dormitory rooms, located in the East Wing of the school.

The Ðorms

According to Warsoma, the East Wing was a far superior location for their dwellings than those given to the other houses. The four wings of the old school were divided into dormitories, all of which had similar layouts. Each dorm was a large, spacious room that was generally shared between four boys. They contained two bunk beds, a desk for each of its occupants and an en-suite bathroom. Each wing had a much larger common room that was used for relaxation and mingling with the other house members. However, as Warsoma had carefully observed, there were subtle differences between the wings, which in his mind at least, had a huge impact on the overall experience.

"Ibn Ajeroom House is located in the North Wing of the school," explained Warsoma, as the boys made their way through the courtyard. "It is always in the shade and therefore it tends to be a dark and gloomy place! As for Abu Hanifa House – its position is in the South Wing, next to the prayer hall. So when the *adhan* for *fajr* is called, it resonates through the walls of their dorms. So you can definitely expect a few to fall out of bed!"

Yusif chuckled to himself at Warsoma's unlikely

57

explanation.

"Really, it can't be all that bad," suggested Yusif, "...besides doesn't everyone hear the call for prayer?"

"Yes, but not quite like them," interrupted Reda, laughing. "The *mu'adhin* may as well be calling the prayer from beside their beds as far as they are concerned! But then again, on the plus side, the rooms were refurbished along with the prayer room last year, so they do look a bit more modern."

Yusif was still not quite convinced, as the whole place looked spectacular to him.

"And what about the West Wing – the residence for Ibn Majah House?" he enquired. Warsoma paused for a second.

"Well, nothing really," he replied thoughtfully. "Except that it's the oldest part of the whole school. Everything is a bit rickety, and there's something strange about it..."

"What do you mean?" asked Yusif, his curiosity aroused.

However, his line of enquiry was cut short. Before Warsoma could answer, they had arrived in front of the beautifully decorated iron door that was the entrance to the East Wing. It was very typical of the style of Moroccan architecture that Yusif had admired around the courtyard. Above the door was an inscription, engraved on a wooden plaque. It read:

'Live for this life as though you will live forever, and live for your hereafter as though you would die tomorrow.'

[Imam Ali]

Yusif read the words. What strange advice! 'We *don't* live forever', he thought to himself. So what did it mean – living life as though you lived forever? But there was no time to ponder the matter further, as the boys were quickly ushered inside by Ustad Ibrahim.

The iron door led into a small lobby. To the right was the common room and to the left was a small kitchen. It was not for the purpose of cooking, reassured Ustad Ibrahim – the boys could hardly be trusted to make their own meals – these would be provided in the canteen. However, it was somewhere they could keep their snacks and drinks – only of the healthy variety, of course.

As they stood in the lobby Yusif looked around, and noticed that the luggage had been brought in from the registration room. It was now sitting piled up to one side. There were cases, trunks and baggage of all varieties. Some were brand new, while others were battered, bruised and had obviously seen better days. He scanned the various items and was relieved to see his own familiar trunk. It was clearly labelled with his name on a large red tag that Ammi had lovingly attached to the side. It read :

'Yusif Abdur-Raheem, Dar Al Ilm Academy, Hastings'

Ustad Ibrahim looked at the boys all gathered around him.

"Now boys, will you all get into groups of four please," he said. "Please bear in mind that those whom you choose will be sharing a dormitory room with you for the rest of the year."

Without a second thought, Yusif, Reda and Warsoma immediately huddled together. Reda, because he was under instructions to look after the newcomer; Warsoma because he and Reda were already good friends, and Yusif because they were the only boys in the whole group that he knew. The other boys followed suit, and before long, they had all grouped together in fours, save the odd straggler who was quickly matched up with a suitable trio.

Ustad Ibrahim perused the groups, quite satisfied with the outcome – that is until he laid eyes on Yusif and his two companions.

"Only three?" he remarked, pausing to look around the room once again. "That's strange, is there anyone else here not part of a group?" he asked. "I'm sure my list was quite evenly divisible by four." But nobody responded.

With that, Ustad Ibrahim shrugged his shoulders and led the group along the long corridor to the dorm rooms. One by one, each group was delivered to their allocated room.

Yusif and his friends had the last room on the ground floor. As anticipated, it was a very large room with two bunk beds, four desks and dark wooden bookshelves lining the walls. There were two windows at the far end with a view looking out onto the courtyard. Upon entering the room, Yusif spent the first few moments staring around and just taking in the space. Looking at the beds, it struck him for the first time as to where he was – *boarding school*. This was it. Like it or not, it was to be his home for the next year.

Reda however, had other things on his mind. Being a veteran of the school, he knew full well what his priority was. Rushing forward, he scrambled up the ladder to the top of one of the bunk beds, and staked his claim.

"Bags my bed!" he shouted triumphantly.

Realising the urgency of the situation, Yusif himself darted forward and leapt up the ladder of the second bunk bed, claiming the top bunk for himself.

"Bags this one!" he proclaimed, not quite as confidently as his predecessor did. Warsoma, who was slower on his feet than the others, was left standing in the middle of the room looking bewildered and at the same time frustrated with his beggar's choice.

"Great!" he complained sarcastically. "So, it's the bottom bunk or the bottom bunk, let me think... which one should I choose?"

"*Ya akhi*, you have to be quicker off the mark!" teased Reda. Sulking, Warsoma walked towards the lower bunk under Reda's bed and threw himself face down on the pillow.

Yusif, who was ever sensitive to other people's feelings, took pity on Warsoma and kindly offered to relinquish his top bunk if Warsoma so wished it. He said that on reflection, he was not as so concerned as to whether he slept at the top or bottom. However, Warsoma was quick to dismiss this generous offer.

"Come to think of it, Yusif," he said looking

smugly back at Reda. "I think I got the better deal!"

"At least I have less distance to fall if I roll off the bed. And also, Reda's won't be the first face I'll see in the morning – now that's what I'd call a rude awakening!"

"Oy!" protested Reda, as he grabbed his pillow and threw it at Warsoma. He ducked in an attempt to avoid the offending article, but ended up head butting it instead. It somehow came to rest on top of his now askew *topee*. Yusif, most entertained by the spectacle, gave out a roar of laughter. Warsoma grabbed the pillow and flung it across the room at Yusif. Missing him abysmally, it landed in front of the half open door – at the feet of *Ustad Ibrahim*, who had just arrived.

Somewhat shocked at the scene that greeted him, Ustad Ibrahim stood in the doorway, shaking his head with disapproval at their antics. Beside him stood a young boy, looking nervously from the pillow fight scene to Ustad Ibrahim. He looked as if he was wondering what he had let himself in for. But Ustad Ibrahim chose to overlook the incident. He coughed discreetly and knocked on the door, seeking permission to enter.

The boys froze at the sight of their housemaster. Jumping off their beds, they stood up straight. Warsoma grabbed the pillow from the floor and returned it to the nearest bed. He welcomed Ustad Ibrahim inside.

"Boys, I'd like to introduce you to Daud – your fourth roommate," he announced. "Daud unfortunately followed the wrong group and found

himself in the Abu Hanifa dorms – didn't you, son?" Ustad Ibrahim asked cheerfully, patting him on the back. Daud nodded his head. He was too nervous in front of his new roommates to be able to speak. Not to mention embarrassed at having made such a silly mistake.

"Well boys, get yourselves settled in and see to it that you help one another," he added. "Oh, and don't forget to collect your luggage from the lobby!" But just as he finished speaking, a loud crash boomed from the hallway.

"*Subhanallah!* What was that noise?" exclaimed Ustad Ibrahim, rushing out into the corridor to investigate the commotion. The boys followed in hot pursuit. Daud however stood rooted to the spot, looking even more bewildered than before, as the others ran past him. It transpired that Zulfiqar Ali had unwisely pulled his baggage out from under the mountainous pile of luggage in the lobby. The ensuing cascade was inevitable, with bags and cases tumbling and crashing down, one after the other.

Having dragged their own cases from the pile, the boys returned to the room, giggling to each other over the excitement outside. In all the commotion Yusif and the boys had forgotten about Daud. Realising the oversight, Yusif turned his attention to the newcomer. He stepped forward with his arms outstretched, warmly grasping Daud's hand in the two of his.

"*Assalaamu alaikum* brother Daud!" he said smiling. "I'm Yusif, this is Warsoma and that's Reda."

"*Wa alaikum assalam,*" replied Daud with a smile.

"I'm Daud, Daud Llewellyn-Jones."

"Llewellyn-Jones?" asked Warsoma. "Where are you from, then?"

He was intrigued by Daud's name, as well as his appearance. Daud was a tallish boy, smartly dressed in the Dar Al Ilm uniform. He had cropped ginger hair, grey eyes and a short freckled nose that wrinkled as he smiled.

"I'm from Aberystwyth. It's a town in west Wales," responded Daud.

"Wales!" interjected Reda, "Oh, that's a fantastic place! We went there last year on a weekend field trip. Erm, where was it? Yes, I remember, Brecon Beacons! That was it! It was so much fun – do you remember Warsoma?"

"How can I forget?" replied Warsoma, pulling a pained expression on his face as he relived the memory of their trip. "I fail to see how hiking up mountains for hours can be described as *fun*," he continued. "It was more like torture! I had blisters on my feet for a long time after!" In fact, he had spent the next few days with his feet soaking in buckets of warm salty water. What an experience!

Daud and Yusif laughed.

"What rubbish!" protested Reda. "Anyway, they weren't mountains, they were hills. It was great. Don't you remember – breathing the fresh air, nature, the elements..."

Warsoma was unmoved.

"Ah yes! You mean trudging through the cold, rain and muddy soil!" Yusif could only imagine what a nightmare the experience must have been for poor Warsoma, who it seemed hated almost every activity related to sport or strenuous exercise.

"The only good thing that came out of that whole trip, was the thousand pounds we raised for charity from the sponsored walk up that *mountain*!" insisted Warsoma.

"Now visiting Caerleon the next day was my kind of trip – the Roman baths, the amphitheatre, the museum..." With that, it was Reda's turn to pull the faces.

"Bor....ing!" moaned Reda, sticking his fingers in his ears. Unimpressed by Reda's childish gestures, Warsoma raised his eyebrows to the sky and turned towards Daud.

Responding to the cue, Daud diplomatically changed the subject.

"I've never been to a boarding school before," he confessed, "what's it like?"

Just like Yusif, he too had no idea what to expect. Likewise, he had been very nervous at the prospect of coming to Dar Al Ilm.

It soon became apparent that Daud's background was quite different to that of Yusif. He explained his story to an eager audience.

His father was a Welshman, who had reverted to Islam some years ago. One of the first things he had wanted to do was to learn Arabic. He was studying at university in those days and with his family responsibilities, it was difficult to achieve his aim. But a few months back, a job offer had come through in the Middle East, which would require him to relocate to an Arabic speaking country. For him, it was like a dream come true!

"And so here I am – packed off to boarding school!" explained Daud throwing his hands up in the air.

"Couldn't you have gone with your parents?" inquired Yusif. Daud shook his head, his freckled nose wrinkling. His parents would have to move around a lot. So they considered it best that he stay behind and go to a boarding school instead. It was not such a difficult choice for them, as they had heard so many good things about Dar Al Ilm Academy.

"Well I'm new here too, so I'm another one who would like to know what boarding school is like," affirmed Yusif, turning towards Reda and Warsoma.

"Yeah, sure no problem," responded Reda. "Let me think, what do you boys need to know?"

With this, he launched into a colourful list of somewhat exaggerated descriptions.

"Well, the dungeons are in the basement – but don't worry, there are plenty of snakes and rats to keep you company! Oh, and you need to watch out for the 'mad' Professor Hakimi – never get on the wrong side of *him*! And whatever you do, never ever go to the North Tower after *maghrib*..."

"Stop teasing, Reda!" laughed Warsoma, elbowing him in the stomach. He grabbed the pillow once more and playfully tossed it towards Reda's face to keep him quiet. Daud and Yusif laughed. Warsoma looked at them, smiling, with dimples across his cheeks.

"Trust me, you'll love it here! But I'll have to tell you over supper, its six o'clock now!" By now he was painfully aware of the fact that he had not managed to grab any of the food which was on offer during registration. "I don't know about you guys, but I'm famished!"

The boys nodded their heads in agreement, and decided that the unpacking could wait until later. With this, the newly acquainted quartet emerged cheerfully from the room. They headed out of the East Wing in the direction of the canteen, with Warsoma at their lead, his tummy rumbling all the way.

Chapter Six

The First Week

It was hard to believe how quickly time flew by at the Academy. A whole week had passed – and what a hectic week it had been! It seemed like only yesterday that Yusif had stepped into the dorm room on the first day of term. It was now Sunday morning, and he had just woken up. Opening his eyes, he lay still for a second, trying to gather his thoughts. As usual, it took him a moment or so to realise he was not at home. He looked over to his right, and smiled as he saw the now familiar sight of Reda fast asleep in his bunk, with his blanket tossed carelessly aside. Every memory of that first week at Dar Al Ilm Academy came flooding back to him...

* * *

On the first evening Yusif, Reda, Warsoma and Daud had enjoyed a delicious supper before returning to unpack their bags. The long day had taken its toll. Travelling in the early hours of the morning and registration had been tiring enough. As for Yusif, the daunting prospect of starting a new school had only added to the exertion. It was no surprise that the boys were exhausted, eager to climb into the comfort of their new beds.

Even Daud was too tired to protest over being left with the lower bunk. In fact, he was only too happy to flop into his bed. But Yusif had found it hard to sleep comfortably, still feeling guilty at taking the top bunk. After all, it was not Daud's fault that he had arrived late at the dorms. He spent a few minutes tossing and turning, before finally hanging his head over the side of the bunk. He looked down at Daud, and asked him if he wanted to swap.

"It's okay – I don't mind taking the lower bunk..." mumbled Daud. "Besides, I'm scared of heights anyway!" With a long yawn, he drifted off to sleep and Yusif shortly followed suit with his conscience much more at ease.

After a hearty breakfast the next morning, the boys' first day began with form class. Timetables were issued and Yusif was quite taken aback at the busy schedule that lay ahead. He was shocked to see that the morning session began after *fajr* prayers, with memorisation of Qur'an for *two hours*! He was slightly relieved to read further:

Hafiz programme – 'optional extra' classes for those interested in memorising the Qur'an. Location : The Prayer Hall.

Of course, the boys did try their level best to attend. After the congregational *fajr* prayer, they stayed behind in the prayer hall. By Thursday, they had been caught snoozing in class two days in a row by Ustad

Ahmad. All four of the boys, along with many other year sevens, were dismissed until such time that they were 'sufficiently settled into their new routines to be able to take the *hafiz* programme more seriously!'

Naturally, Yusif was disappointed, but he realised that Ustad Ahmad was probably quite right in his judgement.

The highlight for Monday was maths. Ustad Nuh, who sniffled for the most part of the lesson, was true to Warsoma's description. The cause of the allergy this time was a gift from Faisal Attia – a fez hat brought back from Turkey. Its dusty tassel had somehow managed to tickle the teacher's nose, sending him into a fit of sneezes.

On Tuesday, science with Ustad Zakariya proved to be very interesting. He turned out to be quite different from many of the other teachers. There was no doubt that he could be very stern, and it seemed apparent that no one was willing to risk getting on the wrong side of him. But Ustad Zakariya was a passionate teacher, and it came across in his teaching. He decided to go easy on the boys in the first week. Much to the relief of his students, he did not launch straight into the science syllabus. Instead, he spent the first couple of lessons describing the contribution of Islam in the field of science and medicine. It was quite a revelation for Yusif and his classmates, who were very surprised at how little they knew about their Islamic heritage.

"Who can tell me who was Al-Razi?" Ustad Zakariya asked.

The question was met with a pin-drop silence. The boys looked from one to another, each hoping that someone else would know the answer. Their blank expressions spoke volumes. Suddenly, hope arose in the form of Musa Akhtar – the boy who had scolded Reda and Warsoma for talking in the prayer hall during the house roll call. He had racked his brains and with a glimmer of inspiration, triumphantly raised his hand aloft. All eyes turned towards him as he sat at the back of the class, grinning like a Cheshire cat. Yusif recalled the scene now vividly, and was not likely to forget it anytime soon!

"Yes, and your name?" enquired Ustad Zakariya as he paused to check against the register.

"Musa Akhtar!" replied the boy, desperate to make a good first impression.

"Yes Musa, your answer if you please," said the teacher.

"Was he the Pharaoh of Egypt?" came the reply.

Ustad Zakariya paused momentarily, frowning his brow in an attempt to make sense of Musa's answer. The sound of sniggering quietly broke out from amongst a few of the boys in the back row. Reda slumped forward on his desk with a sigh of disappointment, realising the unlikelihood of the answer being correct.

It was apparent that Ustad Zakariya was also not at all impressed.

"I think, Musa," he replied shaking his head, "that perhaps you are thinking of *Ramses* – the Pharaoh of Egypt. I spoke of *Al-Razi*, the respected

Muslim physician! He was the first physician in history to describe in detail common illnesses such as measles and the smallpox."

By the end of the class, it was clear to everyone that they would have to work their socks off if they wanted to impress Ustad Zakariya. Especially if they wanted to score points for their respective houses in science!

On Wednesday it was PE. Much to Warsoma's horror, Ustad Hamza did not opt for an easy first week. Accusing the boys of being 'pampered and spoilt over the summer holidays', he had decided that it was time for them to toughen up and get fit! A gruelling cross-country run around the school grounds was the order of the day. It was Yusif's first ever such run, and it left him in *agony*. Every muscle in his body ached by the end of it. Attractive as the grounds may be, he would have preferred to tour at a more leisurely pace.

Thursday was English with Ustad O'Malley. Yusif had never met anyone with such varying degrees of mood. One minute he could be completely laid back without a care in the world. The next minute, he could have a temper fiery enough to match the colour of his red hair! (Yusif only hoped that his new roommate Daud, who was also a red-head, would not turn out to be the same!)

However, in spite of his temperament, Ustad O'Malley could also be very comical at times. He had an apparently endless list of amusing anecdotes, and Yusif liked him very much. Well at least he did, until he became the first teacher to give them homework!

It was all thanks to Sufyan Hamdi, who had recklessly let slip that the class had not been given any homework so far. Ustad O'Malley, was only too happy to make amends for the oversight of his colleagues!

"What! Not overburdened by homework?" Ustad O'Malley had exclaimed in surprise. "Now we can't be having that. Come along now, pens to the paper please!"

And there it was, in black and white – the first entry of the year in their homework diaries. The task, a five hundred word essay on their adventures over the summer holidays! The loud moans of protest from the class could be heard all the way down the school corridor. This was much to the delight of brother Luqman, who was just at that moment passing by their classroom at the time on an errand for his teacher.

It was safe to say that by the end of the week, Yusif had settled down very nicely. He had made firm friends around him in Daud, Warsoma and Reda. Sitting quietly, listening to Sheikh Ansari's *khutbah*, the speech for the Friday prayers, Yusif had felt very much at home at the Academy. A week ago, the boys of year seven who had sat in the rows before and behind him had been complete strangers. Yet now they were faces with familiar names and personalities he was getting to know. Of course, he only knew well the boys from his own house and class 7b (there were three classes in each year, with a mixture of boys from each house). But it was a satisfactory beginning. After all, he had the next thirty-nine weeks to get to know the rest of them!

Warsoma and Reda were in his class, as was Daud, who to Yusif's delight turned out to be a whizz at maths, which was proving to be very handy. More importantly, unlike Ustad O'Malley, he was as cool as a cucumber, despite the red hair! However, there had been one incident during the week that had managed to draw out his temper...One morning at breakfast, Reda had asked Daud for marmalade, addressing him by the words '*ya akhi*'. But poor Daud, not realising the meaning, took great exception to this.

"Can you not call me '*yucky!*'" he had retorted grumpily, "I *have* had a bath you know, and I don't have bad breath either!" At this, Reda burst into laughter. Warsoma, who was sipping a glass of fresh orange juice at the time, choked and began to cough and splutter uncontrollably. That was, until Yusif slapped him firmly on the back.

"I called you *ya akhi* – that's Arabic for brother!" laughed Reda. "Besides, I think we all worked that out, seeing as you spend so long in the shower and keep everyone waiting!" he continued. Daud flushed bright red, but he was quick to see the funny side, and joined in with the laughter.

The class joker in 7b was Adnan Baig. He could do great impersonations and make unusual noises. He was always quacking and hooting, and seemed to know exactly how to put a smile on people's faces – including the teachers. Then there were the twins, Rehan and Farhan Khan, who had the uncanny ability to finish off each other's sentences! Bilal Hafeez was the daydreamer, who always seemed to be gazing out of the class window or be busy doodling on his books. More than once he had been cautioned by the teachers for his lack of attention.

"The answers will be in the book in front of you, not written on the window!" he would be told. The warnings did not seem to have much impact on him, though.

And poor Zulfiqar – he had a gift for creating mayhem. He was one of the clumsiest people Yusif had ever met. The collapsing suitcases on the first night in their dorms was no one-off incident – it was just the beginning! The proceeding days saw his food tray flying across the canteen as he tripped. A pile of text books had fallen off the bookshelf as he pulled out a junior encyclopaedia in science class. And only Allah knows how he had managed to set off the fire alarm, sending the whole school out into the car park halfway through the morning! He had received a firm telling off from Sheikh Ansari himself after that episode.

"Ah well," said the Sheikh at the end of it, exasperated by the young boy's endless mishaps. "At least there would not have to be a fire drill arranged this term!"

Then there was the studious, but very mysterious Azmi Mohamed. He was from Malaysia as Yusif had discovered in Ustad O'Malley's class. A few pupils had been asked to introduce themselves. Azmi had described how he came from the capital city, Kuala Lumpur. He was a quiet type of boy, but clearly intelligent. He kept pretty much to himself – and that was all that anybody knew about him!

When Yusif had chanced upon him in the common room one evening, he had tried to push for a conversation, hoping to draw Azmi out of his shell. Azmi was curled up on a couch with his nose in a book. Yusif dropped down on the couch beside him, and cheerfully asked what he was reading. Azmi looked up, startled and almost dropped his book on his lap. Yusif had never met anyone from Malaysia before and he was very interested in learning about Muslims from another part of the world. He waited curiously for Azmi's reply.

"The Travels of Ibn Batuta," mumbled Azmi, stealing a sideward glance at Yusif, who had hoped that his question would have sparked off a conversation. He was in fact, quite intrigued by the title of the book that his fellow pupil was reading so intently. But Azmi gave a reluctant smile, and continued staring at the pages before him. Yusif pressed him further and asked if it was interesting. Azmi just shrugged his shoulders.

"I guess so, *laa*..." he replied rather disaffectedly, and quickly fell silent once again. It was clear to Yusif that he was not in any mood to talk. He supposed Azmi was either extremely shy, or just terribly homesick. Either way he had decided it would be best to leave him alone for the time being, and try again another day.

Finally, there was Khalid Qureshi, the self-appointed spokesperson for class 7b. He was far too opinionated for his own good. He was particularly unfavoured by Warsoma and Reda, who had known

him since they had started little school together.
Before Khalid had joined Dar Al Ilm, he had travelled
widely throughout the Middle East with his parents
– a fact which he liked to publicise as often as he
could. He described how he had moved from Syria to
Jordan and then Egypt, where his parents had studied
at the famous Al-Azhar University. Khalid considered
himself to be a cut above the rest, though he never
dared to admit this to them openly. He settled for just
imposing his views on others with the understanding
that 'he knew best'.

Khalid's attitude did not go down well with
Warsoma or Reda. For instance, last year on the
weekend field trip to Wales, the boys had been
allowed to explore the Roman Museum in Caerleon.
As they walked around the Roman baths, they had
admired the beautifully decorated mosaic patterns,
with their colourful array of small square tiles.
They were amazed at the great achievements of the
mighty Roman Empire. Khalid took it upon himself
to assume the role of curator, and talked them through
the history of the Romans. He informed them at
length about the rise of the Roman Empire and its
dramatic fall at the hands of the Muslim armies
in Constantinople.

It was not that Khalid's monologue was
uninteresting. It was just the way he spoke to them,
rather condescending and arrogant. Warsoma had
cringed all the way through. As for poor Reda – it put
him into an extra bad mood. For him, it was the double
blow of firstly visiting 'another boring museum',

and secondly for having to listen to 'Mr know it all!' His agitation had come to a head by the time they had left the museum to walk around the old ruins of the Caerleon amphitheatre. Had it been still functioning, Reda had thought to himself, he would have been first to throw Khalid on to the floor of the amphitheatre and feed him to the lions!

"*Astaghfirullah!*" Reda muttered to himself, coming to his senses. What an awful thought! His mother was right – he had to learn to have patience with others, even if they annoyed him, like Khalid quite often did!

His mother was full of sound advice for him.

"Rise above it Reda, and behave in the best of manners with patience, like the blessed Prophet Muhammad did," she had often warned. "Otherwise you may lose your way and become sinful!" And she was right!

It was fair to say that Warsoma and Reda were two very headstrong characters. After the trip, they had each privately felt that Khalid needed to be brought down a peg or two. By the end of the first week of year seven, it was also an opinion that came to be privately held by Yusif, Daud and the rest of class 7b!

Chapter Seven

The Fig Tree

After *jumah* prayer, Sheikh Ansari cancelled afternoon class for year seven, which gave them an early start to the weekend. Of course, this went down very well with the boys. They were free to explore the school, play sports, have a dip in the school swimming pool or just relax in their dorms.

At Reda's suggestion Yusif, Daud, Warsoma and a few other boys had decided to go down to the Lower Fields to play a game of cricket. Warsoma as always, averse to all things sporting, only agreed after a great deal of coaxing from the others. The alternative would have been to spend the afternoon alone in the dorm.

"Besides, it's too sunny to be cooped up inside," argued Yusif. "Just have one game with us, and after that we can explore, or do whatever you like!" Yusif's words had the desired effect. So the next two hours were spent in the happy pursuit of scoring runs, counting overs and very loud yells of 'howzat?'

Reda was a committed sports enthusiast. It was most entertaining for Yusif and Daud to watch his unbridled zeal. On one occasion, Bilal had hit the ball out into the covers where Warsoma had chosen to stand. Warsoma had especially selected the spot, figuring that the further away he stood, the less likely it would be that he would have to do anything. He could not have been further from the truth. At the time, he was busy looking at a starling that had landed just a few yards from him. His attention was suddenly diverted, as Daud screamed at the top of his voice, waving his hands frantically.

"Warsoma! The ball! The ball!" he shouted. "Turn around, it's heading your way – you have to catch it!"

Warsoma spun round with a look of sheer terror on his face. His eyes fixed upon the red leather-bound ball, which was soaring through the air towards him like a blazing fireball. His legs stood rooted to the ground, as he nervously clasped his hands together praying desperately that he would catch it.

"*Akhi*! what are you doing?" screamed Reda as he abandoned his position and ran towards the quivering Warsoma. With a feeble last minute attempt to make the catch, Warsoma opened the palms of his hands, and shut his eyes as tight as he could. But it was too late. The ball struck him on the shoulder and he fell to the ground flat on his back.

After a few moments lying still, Warsoma slowly opened his eyes, half dazed by the impact. Yusif and Daud were standing over him. He sat up slowly, rubbing his shoulder to ease the dull ache. Reda, who was panting for breath, having sprinted across the field, dropped down beside him.

"Is he okay?" he asked, turning his head to look at Daud and Yusif.

"I think so..." replied Daud, "he just had the wind

knocked out of him!"

"Warsoma you goose! You're not supposed to close your eyes and pray you'll catch the ball!" moaned Reda. "You pray, then stick your hands out and trust in Allah that you'll catch it! I can't believe it, we lost!"

Reda sulked dreadfully. He picked up the offending article, which lay motionless beside Warsoma, and threw it off into the far distance.

Zulfiqar, who was watching nearby suddenly doubled over and burst into a fit of laughter at the sight of his wounded classmate.

"What's so funny, Zulfi? I can't remember you catching the ball in any innings. Come here you *butterfingers*!" cried Reda as he jumped to his feet. He turned and ran in hot pursuit of poor Zulfiqar, who was fast fleeing across the Lower Fields, desperate to reach the safety of his dorm room!

"You two are so funny," laughed Yusif stretching out his hand to help Warsoma to his feet. "One minute you fight, the next minute you're the best of friends. It's so funny that Reda teases you himself, but he gets so protective of you when you're teased by others!"

Warsoma pulled himself up and brushed the grass off his clothes. He looked rather disappointed at the large green stain smeared across his left shoulder.

"Oh, he doesn't really mean it!" replied Warsoma. "He's like a big brother. He looks out for me – he always has...It is funny I guess. We *are* a bit like chalk and cheese!" Suddenly Warsoma looked up at Yusif. He forgot about the grass stains for a moment, and a look of guilt appeared upon his face.

"But Reda was right this time," confessed Warsoma. "He's not angry because I missed the ball. I should have tied my camel!"

Daud looked confused.

"I don't understand," he said. "What's tying a camel got to do with playing cricket?"

"No *akhi*," laughed Yusif. "He is talking about one of the sayings of the Prophet Muhammad, peace be upon him. One day, the Prophet noticed a bedouin leaving his camel without tying it and he asked the bedouin why he didn't tie his camel." Yusif gestured with hands, as though he was tying an imaginary rope. He continued his explanation.

"The bedouin replied, 'I put my trust in Allah.' The Prophet then said, 'Tie your camel first, then put your trust in Allah'. I know this saying like the back of my hand. Abu is forever reminding me of the Prophet's words, especially when he thinks I'm being lazy!"

"Do you see now?" interjected Warsoma. "I prayed to catch it. But I didn't actually make any effort to try. I couldn't see past the vision of that 'fireball' burning a hole right through the palms of my hands!" Warsoma laughed, shaking his head at his own foolish thoughts.

Daud was half listening. He was still pondering at the Prophet's words.

"Wow! I've never thought about it like that before," he said. "I'm always praying for things, but not actually doing anything towards earning them!"

"Well, now you know!" responded Warsoma. "So that essay Ustad O'Malley gave us isn't going to write itself and get you an 'A' grade. We have to really try hard and put our best efforts into it. The result is up to Allah."

"Oh no, don't remind me! I hate English. Give me fractions any day!" complained Daud, shaking his head as he pondered on the essay that loomed before him. "I don't know what to write about!"

In the meantime, a dark blanket of cloud had appeared in the sky above them. The boys had not noticed it until the cool droplets of water pricked against their faces.

"Well, we won't get inspiration standing here under the rain in Lower Fields!" said Yusif glancing at the sky above suspiciously. "C'mon, we should get back, and besides we need to look in on Zulfi, Reda was looking awfully angry!"

They raced back towards the East Wing, covering their heads from the rain with their arms. Before long, they burst into the common room, momentarily disturbing the peace. They were damp and quite chilled from the downpour.

Azmi was sitting as usual with his nose in a book. Harun Gibbs and Muhammad Diwan, or 'Hamudi' as he was better known, were busy on the far side of the room near the windows, absorbed in a game of Scrabble. Yusif, Warsoma and Daud headed straight for the fireplace, its hot embers glowing. The flames danced and flickered brightly, as they sat huddled together in front of them. It was not long before the warmth embraced them, replacing their shivers with relief and comfort.

They were still chatting away about their essays when Reda walked in and threw himself down on one of the armchairs near the fireplace. Yusif was the first to speak, very curious to find out what had happened to poor Zulfi.

It transpired that Reda, having chased Zulfi across the Lower Fields, had arrived at the dorms in a far better mood than before. The strenuous run had soothed his temperament considerably. Nevertheless, poor Zulfi, who was completely unaware of Reda's change in mood, had rushed into his dorm room and locked himself in. Utterly terrified, he was convinced that Reda meant to play some mean trick on him.

Fortunately for him, his roommate Amar Hasan was in the room with him. He had spent a peaceful afternoon writing to his friends and family back home, and was winding down with a favourite book. For his part, he had no intention of spending the next few hours barricaded in his room. Amar tried his best to reason with the desperate Zulfi, explaining that he could not avoid Reda forever! After all, they had to eat and he could not possibly see how Zulfi expected to go unnoticed, or skip class. Eventually Zulfi saw sense.

Reda was stood outside, his arms folded across his chest, looking very cross over the events of the afternoon. He was frustrated, and having knocked three times according to Islamic etiquette, had been about to walk away. At that moment, Zulfi opened the door. He popped his head cautiously around it, looking very much frightened. His dark brown eyes widened with a sense of doomed anticipation.

Upon seeing Zulfi's petrified expression, Reda softened. In fact, under that tough demeanour he was really a 'big softie' at heart, as Warsoma was often quick to point out. Reda unfolded his arms and coughed uncomfortably.

"Zulfi, I...erm, I just came to apologise," he stammered. "I shouldn't have chased you. And it was very wrong of me to have spoken to you as I did. After all it was only a silly game!"

Reda held out his hand as a gesture of good will. Zulfi blinked his eyes half in amazement, as he gazed upon the outstretched hand. He was a little dumbfounded by the unexpected response. Amar, who was standing close behind Zulfi, was eager to see what would transpire between the two of them. He gave a discreet nudge, which prompted Zulfi to accept the apology.

"I'm sorry too...that I laughed at Warsoma," he said, much relieved. "It was very wrong of me as well. Oh, and I'll apologise to Warsoma too when I see him next!"

Pleased to have avoided having his ears boxed, Zulfi made a mental note never to provoke Reda again. He would have to learn to hold his unruly tongue!

It was after the successful reconciliation that Reda had returned to the common room and cheerfully greeted Yusif, Warsoma and Daud, who were by then sprawled out over the sofa in front of the fire. He quickly assured Yusif and the other boys that Zulfi was not only happy, but still in one piece. And no, he was not upset with Warsoma, or over the fact that they had lost the game. He was just fine. After all, it was only a silly game anyway.

"What are you going to write about for Ustad O'Malley's essay?" asked Daud, eager to return to the subject they had been discussing earlier. Reda suddenly sat forward, very much animated.

"Oh, I meant to tell you after the class finished, but I completely forgot!" he said, full of excitement. "You'll never guess what I did over the hols – I visited the town of Nawa, where Imam Al Nawawi lived, a long time ago."

All three boys looked at Reda, intrigued. His words also caught the attention of the other boys who were sitting in the common room. Harun, Hamudi and in particular Azmi, pricked up their ears.

"Who's Imam Al Nawawi?" asked Harun. Warsoma frowned.

"Who *was* Imam Al Nawawi?" he said rhetorically, throwing his hands up in the air. "Only one of the greatest Islamic scholars that ever lived..."

Most of the boys had heard of the famous scholar Imam Al Nawawi. Sheikh Ahmed had dedicated an entire assembly last term to the life of this great figure from Islamic history.

"I thought you went to Jordan, isn't Imam Al Nawawi's town in Syria?" asked Warsoma, looking a little puzzled.

"I did – at first," explained Reda. "But my parents decided to go on to Syria and visit some relatives. Uncle Mohiyudeen took us on a *ziyarah*. It was a tour of the historical sites in and around the city of Damascus."

"We went to Bosra and saw the house of the Christian monk Bahira," continued Reda. "He was the one who recognised the seal of prophethood on Messenger's back when he was a child." He pointed to the back of his shoulder, showing where the mark would have been. "The Prophet was visiting Syria with his uncle at the time."

"After that, we went to the town of Nawa, to visit a friend of my uncle's. This friend took us around the old town, which was Imam Al Nawawi's birthplace, and also where he is buried. That was a *very* interesting place..."

"Wow, Imam Al Nawawi!" gasped Warsoma, very much impressed.

"What do you mean it was a very interesting place?" asked Yusif, intrigued by Reda's description. His enthusiasm prompted further explanation from Reda.

"Well, we stood outside the old stone mausoleum, which had been built around Imam Al Nawawi's grave," he continued. "But there was no dome or roof, as you may have seen in other places. Instead all you could see was some twisted branches of a tree that stood at the centre of the mausoleum, towering high over the walls..." Reda, twisted and wound his arms in the air, as he demonstrated the shape of the branches.

"When we went inside through a rusty old iron gate, we found no tomb, just a giant tree standing at the centre!" The boys looked at one another before staring back at Reda, fascinated by his description.

"Are you sure you had the right place?" asked Daud.

"Well it *was* the right place, actually!" retorted Reda. "Imam Al Nawawi's grave was under the tree!" The boys exchanged confused looks.

"Are you teasing?" asked Warsoma with a smirk, as he carefully studied Reda's face, half-expecting to see that all too familiar twinkle in his eyes – or some other tell-tale sign that proved he was just pulling their legs.

"Akhi, I'm serious!" assured Reda, solemnly placing his hand on his chest. Warsoma raised his eyebrow sceptically, and folded his arms. He was not going to be duped by Reda!

"I know I'll prove it!" exclaimed Reda as he jumped to his feet and ran out of the common room. His colleagues looked at one another bemused. Exactly how did he intend to prove it? It's not like he could bring the mausoleum here, thought Yusif to himself.

After a few moments, Reda returned. As he entered the room all eyes fell on a white envelope that he was clutching tightly in his hand. Dropping down onto the armchair once again, he looked around at his eagerly attentive friends. His eyes shone – how pleased he was that he had remembered to pack the photographs he had taken on his travels.

"I have a picture to prove it! I had taken it before I realised where we were," he announced smugly. The boys gathered around him, including Azmi, Hamudi and Harun who had abandoned their books and games and now were overcome with curiosity.

Reda carefully searched through the photos. There were various pictures of mosques, breathtaking desert landscapes, colourful *souks* and a variety of interesting scenes from that part of the world.

Before long, he found the photo he was looking for. The picture showed the outside of the mausoleum, standing firm on top of a hill with an old stony path leading to it. The walls were set in rows of alternating grey and white stones. And sure enough, just as Reda had described, there was no dome or roof. Just a solitary tree towering firmly above the old stone walls, with twisted and crooked branches spreading over them.

"*Subhanallah*! It does look odd," exclaimed Yusif. He was standing behind Reda looking over his shoulder at the picture. It was a sentiment shared by all the boys, as they scrutinised the photograph, not realising that all fig trees, which is what it was, naturally have such an appearance.

"There was an old man sitting by the grave," continued Reda. "He was the caretaker, a local man from the town of Nawa. He told us about Imam Al Nawawi's life..."

Reda pointed to the lower branches of the tree near the ground. They were covered with lush green leaves, which was in stark contrast to the taller, bare branches that seemed to tower above.

"When Imam Al Nawawi died, he was buried in this place. But he was so loved and respected by the people of Nawa, over time they decided to build

a mausoleum above his grave. But every time they came to put a dome on the building, it fell down – and this happened more than once!"

The boys sat wide-eyed, curiously listening as the story unfolded.

"Well, what did they do?" cried Harun impatiently. Reda grinned, enjoying his moment of being at the centre of everyone's attention.

"Yes, do tell us, before your head gets any bigger!" added Warsoma. He was every bit as anxious as the others were, but was only too aware of Reda's inflating ego.

"Okay! Okay!" laughed Reda. "Well, the old man said that eventually a dome *did* manage to survive. But one day a fig tree sprouted up. It grew and grew until its branches toppled the dome over. The tree's branches spread over the mausoleum in such a fashion, that it became impossible to rebuild the dome ever again!"

"I don't get it," said Hamudi with some confusion in his tone. "So what if a tree grew – is that such a big deal?" he asked. At this point Azmi, known up until now in the house as 'the quiet one', interjected. It so happened that the Imam was something of a hero to him!

"Well, Imam Al Nawawi considered that it was wrong to build over a grave..." said Azmi, with some enthusiasm in his voice. "My father told me!" he continued.

Yusif smiled, looking curiously at Azmi. This was the first time anyone had seen Azmi so animated.

"You're right!" said Reda, suitably impressed by Azmi's knowledge.

"*Subhanallah!*" exclaimed Daud.

"You can say that again!' said Reda, as he proceeded to relate a short biography of Imam Al Nawawi. The great scholar had been dedicated to Islam, spending his whole life studying and teaching. He wrote a great many books.

After Reda's brief description, the audience was captivated. Sensing their intrigue, he paused dramatically. Leaning forward in his armchair, he lowered his voice to a whisper. "The old man told us that people of the town used to say that because Imam Al Nawawi was so pious, Allah allowed his view to come to pass. The gigantic tree grew, expanding from day to day. In a way, it was just like his knowledge, which has spread far and wide. It benefits the Muslims even until now..."

"I don't know about that," protested Warsoma shaking his head vigorously. "It's all superstitious nonsense! Muslims do not believe in superstitions and fairytale stories! Next you'll be saying the tooth fairy is real!" exclaimed Warsoma. He paused for a moment as a sudden mischievous thought entered his head.

"Erm, you do know that's not true?" asked Warsoma his eyes twinkling. Hamudi and Harun looked at each other and grinned.

"Don't be daft, of course there's no such thing as the tooth fairy. And yes I know it's all superstitious nonsense!"

"Good. It's just a tree! And why shouldn't it grow

there anyway, it's as good a place as any other!" pronounced Warsoma feeling rather full of sense and logic. Reda groaned in frustration. Really, Warsoma could be quite exasperating at times.

"The point of the story," said Reda looking at Warsoma patiently, "was to show how immensely loved and respected he was as one of the greatest scholars in Islamic history. It may not have been a particularly attractive tree to look at, but it was definitely a healthy tree, full of *barakah*! The old man said at one time it produced figs in so much abundance that it fed the entire town!"

"I don't like figs," said Harun wrinkling his nose up in disgust, " – too many seeds! Always get stuck between your teeth. Now dates with warm milk and honey, *mmm...delicious!*" he exclaimed kissing the tips of his fingers.

"*Subhanallah*, nothing lives or grows without Allah's permission!" reflected Azmi as he imagined the townsfolk harvesting the fruits of the tree on a hot summer's day. Personally, he rather liked figs, especially when his grandmother turned them into sweet chutney, as she did for special occasions like Eid – or *Hari Raya* as it is known in Malaysia. It was a secret recipe, handed down to her by her own grandmother.

"My father told me once, that most people don't realise how amazing Imam Al Nawawi was," said Azmi returning to the subject of Imam Al Nawawi. "Did you know that he completed his studies in a very short space of time? He studied in his youth and started writing from the age of thirty until he died at the age of just forty five. He produced a huge number of important Islamic works!" explained Azmi with much admiration.

"So, that's why you're such a bookworm!" laughed Yusif, making Azmi blush to the roots of his hair. Sensing his embarrassment, Yusif quickly commended him on his enthusiasm, especially as this was the first time that Azmi had come out of his shell.

Nevertheless, far from feeling teased, Azmi was really quite pleased. Yusif's comments had made him warm towards him. After his last encounter with Yusif in the common room when he had tried to talk to him, Azmi could not help but like him.

He had really regretted having given Yusif the cold shoulder. It was not at all like him to be so discourteous. However, since coming to the Academy, Azmi had deliberately distanced himself from everyone. It was a form of retaliation for being sent to the school. When his parents had 'packed him off' to boarding school in a foreign country, he had felt betrayed, and had made up his mind not to like it.

With a combination of homesickness and anger, he just had not been able to bring himself to speak to anyone. Instead, he had chosen to spend most of his time wallowing away in self-pity. This was the first time he had made any effort to talk to any of the Academy boys. And quite frankly he was relieved. He had grown sick and tired of his self-imposed isolation. After all it was obvious to him now that he was not going to see home for a while, as his parents had told him so. Yes, Azmi was quite relieved. At last, he had broken his silence!

"Imam Al Nawawi never wasted a moment," he continued. "He literally lived in the library of Damascus for two years. They say he was always reading. He wouldn't even sleep in his bed. When he got tired, he just put his head down over a book, took a nap and then continued to read when he woke up!"

"Hey, I must be in good company!" interrupted Reda, unable to resist. "I'm always falling asleep over my books!" At this, the boys all burst into a fit of laughter – with the exception of Warsoma, who was quick to point out the real cause – laziness and lack of attention!

"Well, I wouldn't go writing about Imam Al Nawawi's sleeping habits in your essay Reda!" said Daud rather seriously. "Knowing Ustad O'Malley as we do now, he might think we have it too easy at school altogether! The next thing you know, we'll be told lessons actually shouldn't end at all!" There were groans all round from the gathered boys, which soon turned to laughter at the thought of waking up to the sight of Ustad O'Malley, handing out assignments in the dorms at *fajr* time.

And so it was for the rest of the evening, that the sound of laughter could be heard more than once coming from the Ibn Kathir House common room.

"They always settle in..." chuckled Ustad Ibrahim to Ustad Nuh, as they walked together past the common room door later that evening, overhearing the commotion.

"In these past ten years, I've never had a boy who hasn't – not on my watch!"

—— Chapter Eight ——

Yusif's Talent

"Now remember!" remarked Ustad Ibrahim sternly, "The middle part of the throat lies halfway between the beginning and the end." He pointed his index finger at the centre of his neck, and then directed the gathered pupils towards a cross-section diagram of the mouth, which hung on the wall behind him. This was Yusif's first lesson in the 'Science of *Tajweed*' at Dar Al Ilm, and it was quite different to what he had been used to with his old Qur'an teacher back in Birmingham.

The session began with a ritual 'vocal training exercise', as Ustad Ibrahim called it. He would start by describing some of the theory behind how the letters of the Arabic alphabet were pronounced, and then instruct the pupils to practise the letters. He considered it a prerequisite for the class – for the benefit of the beginners, as well as those who felt themselves more experienced in the subject.

"But, sir..." moaned Hamudi, rather ungraciously. "Most of us know our letters, especially those from little school!" Ustad Ibrahim peered over his glasses in his usual serious manner, and looked straight at Hamudi who was sitting at the back of the class.

"Young man, it is essential that the Qur'an is read with the correct pronunciation of the letters and vowels," explained Ustad Ibrahim gravely. "One slight error and you may have changed the whole meaning completely!"

"Besides, pronouncing the letters and vowels is not as easy as you might think – it takes time to perfect this skill!"

"I'm well aware that many of you may know your letters – and some of you are even quite proficient in recitation. Nevertheless, the more practice you get of the basics – the better! Especially for those of you who are not Arabs, as you may not be familiar with the sounds of certain letters in the Arabic language. Even some of you who *are* Arabs have become quite lazy with your pronunciation!"

And so it was for the weeks that followed, lessons in the science of *tajweed* would meticulously cover every letter, vowel and punctuation mark in the Arabic language.

In one particular lesson, it was a warm Wednesday afternoon, and the bright sunlight came flooding into the room. The windows had been opened and the thick scent of incense from the courtyard drifted in on the cool breeze from the Hastings seacoast. Yusif sat at his usual desk in the front row with Warsoma beside him to the right and Daud to his left. Reda, who was ever keen to keep away from the direct and watchful gaze of Ustad Ibrahim, conveniently sat behind the other three. All eyes were fixed on the teacher's finger, which moved from his throat to the illustrated diagram of the mouth.

"The two letters that are emitted from here are; *'ha'* and *'ayn'*. Now altogether, let's say *'ayn!'*" A dreadful chorus of *'ayn'* filled the classroom. Sheikh Ibrahim shook his head, half in amusement and half in despair.

"Good attempt boys – but try to sound a little less like donkeys!" laughed Ustad Ibrahim heartily.

"Now I would like you to get into groups and practise for a few minutes the letters articulated from the part of the throat closest to the mouth; *'gha'* and *'kha'*" ordered Ustad Ibrahim.

Reda pulled his chair forward to sit with Yusif, Warsoma and Daud who were by then sat poking their fingers against their necks, producing a wide range of weird and wonderful strangled sounds.

"You all look and sound silly!" laughed Reda. Daud looked exasperated. This was not one of his strongest subjects and his throat was positively sore.

"I, I just can't do it!" replied Daud, drumming his fists on his desk with frustration.

"Sure you can, it's like someone's choking you – see!" laughed Reda as he grabbed Daud's throat and pretended to throttle him. Daud burst into a fit of giggles.

"Stop, that tickles!" spluttered Daud, "...and your hands are so cold! Okay! Let me try again!" Daud composed himself and took a deep breath.

"khaa!"

"That's it – spot on I'd say!" replied Yusif patting him on the back. "You just have to stop spitting now!"

Yusif and the boys broke into laughter.

"Yeah, I love you for the sake of Allah *akhi*, but that does not extend to your sputum!" said Warsoma, grimacing in disgust as he removed his glasses to wipe clean the spray of spit that had coated his lenses.

"*Khalas*! I think that's enough now!" interrupted Ustad Ibrahim. "Everyone back to your places!"

Once the boys had all returned to their places, shuffling their chairs back to their former positions, the room fell silent. Ustad Ibrahim looked thoughtfully at the boys, stroking his white beard in his hand. After a few moments he looked up at the clock above the classroom door and shook his head – his mind was made up.

"Since you have all been working so hard these past weeks, and we have a few minutes to spare till the end of class, we shall listen to some recitation of the Qur'an from a few of you!" The class suddenly buzzed with excitement.

"So, do I have any volunteers?"

Reda sunk down in his seat as he heard Ustad Ibrahim's request, earnest in the hope that Yusif's small person was adequate to shield him from the teacher's watchful gaze. He sighed with relief as the familiar hand of Hamudi shot up eagerly, at the back of the class. Peering over his glasses, Ustad Ibrahim smiled.

"Yes Muhammad – if you please, stand up. Recite from the beginning of the book, *bismillah*..."

Hamudi stood up and opened the Qur'an carefully to the front page. It was the first chapter, *al-Fatihah*,

'The Opening'. He smiled nervously as he looked at Ustad Ibrahim. He was suddenly overcome by a feeling of regret at his eagerness to read. Ustad Ibrahim stood by Hamudi's desk, his eyes closed in deep concentration, as he waited for the recitation to begin. Hamudi gulped, took a deep breath and opened his mouth to sound the first letter.

"*Bi* – "

"Shh!" interrupted Ustad Ibrahim shaking his head gravely. "*Isti'adha*! You must always begin recitation of the Qur'an with seeking refuge in Allah!" he continued with his eyes still very much closed.

And so it was that Hamudi continued to recite the first chapter *al-Fatihah*, with continuous interruptions from Ustad Ibrahim as he corrected the poor boy's many mistakes. From forgetting to make the sound of the Arabic letter *lam* heavy when it appeared in Allah's name, right through to the last line of the chapter when he struggled with joining the sounds of the Arabic letters *daad* to *lam* correctly.

Poor Hamudi! By the end of the chapter he was evidently flustered, but relieved to have finished. The task had been a lot harder than he had thought it would be. Feeling very disappointed Hamudi closed the Qur'an and slumped back in his chair.

Ustad Ibrahim opened his eyes to look at Hamudi in surprise. "That was a commendable first attempt. You should be very pleased with yourself!"

"Sir? But I was terrible – I struggled all the way through!" replied Hamudi, much puzzled by Ustad Ibrahim's feedback.

"Ah – but because of your struggle, your reward is twice as great as the one who reads it beautifully and correctly!" assured Ustad Ibrahim. "Remember the saying of the Prophet Muhammad, peace be upon him, 'He who recites the Qur'an well and clearly is equal in rank to the Angels who record creation's deeds. These Angels are gracious, honourable and of lofty rank. He who finds difficulty in reciting the Qur'an will obtain a double reward.'"

Upon hearing these wise words, Hamudi cheered up instantly, his face beaming with smiles.

"Now who would like to read next?"

The next to read was Khalid, and as Yusif expected, the recitation was very good. He was so fluent that he managed to read chapter one and the first page of chapter two, *al-Baqarah*, 'The Cow', with very few mistakes. Ustad Ibrahim was much pleased with his effort. Khalid who was every bit as pleased with himself, grinned smugly and leaned back on his chair.

Warsoma was next, and he read chapter one very reasonably, as did Azmi after him.

"I think..." said Ustad Ibrahim glancing once more at the clock on the wall, "yes...we have time for just one more. So who would like to go next?"

The boys sat silently. Heads turned eagerly in the direction of their neighbours, as each boy hoped that someone else would step forward. Having listened to the previous four boys, it had become apparent to everyone that reciting the Qur'an was not as easy as they had thought it was going to be. Zulfi sat with his head bent forward, as if for some reason suddenly mesmerised by his polka dot pencil case.

In fact, wild horses would not make him volunteer to read. Especially not after listening to Khalid. Although he had spent years of after-school lessons with Aunty Zaynab learning to recite Qur'an, it was now clear to him that what he had just heard was very different to how Aunty had taught him!

"Well now, what happened to all the enthusiasm?" laughed Ustad Ibrahim.

"Never mind, let me see – Ah! Yusif would you care to read?"

Yusif nearly jumped out of his seat when he heard his name called out. Full of nerves, he nodded his head, unable to refuse the Ustad's kindly gaze. He fumbled for the Qur'an that lay on his desk and slowly stood up. All of a sudden, Yusif became acutely conscious of the many eyes upon him. Although utterly terrified, he began to recite, a little shakily at first.

But as his tongue twisted around the familiar sounds, he gained momentum. His heart, previously pounding at a thousand beats per minute, slowed to match the rhythmic recitation. Losing himself in the beautiful words of the Qur'an, he imagined he was back in his beloved teacher's study. He recalled the picture of Ustad Mustafa, sitting at his desk with his favourite herbal tea beside him, filling the air with its fruity aroma, his head swaying from side to side as he listened intently to the sound of Yusif's voice.

"Bzzz – " The sound of the school buzzer pierced

through the air, bringing Yusif abruptly back to the reality of the moment. He blinked at the page in front of him, then gasped suddenly as he realised that he had read as far as the third page of chapter two. But why had no one stopped him? He closed the Qur'an, bringing it slowly to his lips in the traditional sign of respect for the Book of Allah. He looked up. The answer to his question became all too clear! It was written upon the face of each and every one of the people around him.

Yusif was stunned by his captive audience. Ustad Ibrahim was comfortably seated on his chair, beaming with satisfaction. Warsoma who was sat beside him, stared in awe, his mouth almost agape.

"Mashallah!" And that was all Ustad Ibrahim said, before calmly dismissing the class.

Outside in the corridor, Yusif was mobbed by his classmates.

"Well – aren't you a dark horse!" declared Warsoma, still stunned by what he had heard from his friend. "I'd never have guessed it, looking at you!"

"What, I don't know what you mean! Guessed what?" asked Yusif, puzzled by the reactions of the other pupils, who one by one came over and patted him on his back.

"That if anyone was going to out-do Khalid in recitation – it would be you!" replied Warsoma holding tightly on to his books amidst all the pushing and shoving. Yusif was still confused.

"You mean, you think I'm better than Khalid?" asked Yusif incredulously, "I don't think so! He recited beautifully, *mashallah*..."

"Trust me *akhi*, Khalid is good *mashallah* – but you are really, really, really, good, *mashallah*!" assured Warsoma, shaking Yusif by the shoulders. Just then, Reda and Daud came bursting through the crowds.

"Did you see Khalid's face?" exclaimed Reda. "He looked like he was going to pull off his *topee* and eat it – he was so mad! Yusif, you're a genius!"

Daud was just about to add his own comments, when he suddenly stopped. Just then, Luqman came rushing around the corner. A wave of gasps and whispers emanated from the crowd of boys, reverberating across the length of the corridor.

"It's Luqman – It's Luqman! Quick, let's get out of here!" cried one boy.

"Oh no, he's got the misdemeanour book!" cried another, as he headed briskly in the opposite direction.

"Okay, you all know the rules!" cried Luqman waving the curious old red leather-bound book in the air. "Corridors should be cleared at break times – everyone out!" blasted Luqman, not at all impressed by the crush.

With this, Yusif and the boys quickly made their way out into the courtyard, and headed towards the water fountain. It was Daud who was first to reach it, and he laughed as he turned to look back at the crowd.

"What was that all about?"

"Mr Meany Mark!" said Warsoma as he came up behind Daud, shortly followed by Reda and Yusif.

"Mista – what? " asked Daud .

"Luqman was holding the misdemeanour book, you see. Anyone caught breaking school rules is registered in the book. At the end of the day, Sheikh Ansari looks at the book. If he considers the action very bad, he gives out a misdemeanour or 'Mr Meany Mark' as we call it. That's a point deducted from your house score!"

"Oh!" replied Daud, his eyes widening with surprise. He had never taken Luqman very seriously until now. On first impressions, he had thought of him as nothing but an 'old bossy boots' who liked to think he was in charge of everyone. Chewing his lower lip as he did when something bothered him, Daud looked back at the crowd of boys. Luqman was there, eagerly pencilling in the names of two boys who had gotten into an argument in the corridor after a mix up with their coats. He sighed with relief, grateful to have escaped the pages of the book.

Suddenly Daud's attention shifted away from Luqman's disciplinary antics. Khalid was making his way through the gathered boys, heading straight in their direction.

"Uh-oh! Khalid's coming this way," said Daud, "and he doesn't look very happy!"

"No prizes for guessing what he wants to speak to you about, Yusif!" grinned Reda as he jumped up to sit on the mosaic-tiled wall that surrounded the water fountain. It was from there that he hoped to gain a better view of the spectacle that was no doubt to ensue.

Yusif looked surprised.

"I can't see why he should want to speak to me now. It's not like we've exchanged many words before," said Yusif, suddenly overwhelmed with a feeling of unease.

"Yes, but it's different now. You're his competition!" responded Reda, folding his arms across his chest with the satisfaction of seeing Khalid thus challenged by the newcomer.

"For what?" asked Yusif, somewhat taken aback by the statement.

"Khalid wants to be year captain – you did know that, didn't you?" asked Warsoma, surprised and amused by Yusif's naivety. Yusif stared blankly at Warsoma for a second, before the full comprehension of his words sunk in.

"You mean me...as year captain?" Yusif burst out laughing, tears welling in his eyes. But his laughter was short lived, as he realised he was the only one amused by what he thought to be such a ridiculous notion. Both Warsoma and Daud stood with their arms folded, looking decidedly unimpressed by Yusif's response.

Yusif cleared his throat uncomfortably. "I don't think so!" he replied defensively.

"Why not?" asked Reda bluntly. Disturbed by his friend's lack of enthusiasm, he jumped off the wall and turned his full attention towards Yusif.

Yusif could not answer. There were thousands of reasons as far as he was concerned. In his mind, being the year captain would mean you would have to be pretty special – someone like Abdul Kadir! From his point of view, it was a ridiculous idea for someone like him, and a new boy at that, to be year captain!

"Well, why not?" asked Reda, breaking in on Yusif's thoughts, as he stood silent. Reda looked quite cross. His shoulders were pulled back as he stood straight up to his full height. It was a pose he adopted when he meant business. It worked! Yusif was cornered, and moved to answer rather reluctantly.

"Well, for a start – I have never done anything like that in my whole life, and I wouldn't know what to do. I'm sure there are more clever people than me, and better suited to..."

"Well you're wrong there!" interjected Warsoma. "You're clever, but more importantly the year captain has to be good with people, and good at Qur'an recitation. And you are one of the best in our year – right guys?"

Warsoma looked to the others for support, which he got in an instant. All nodded and agreed unanimously. But before anything could be discussed further, the group fell silent as Khalid joined them by the fountain.

He was not alone. Standing beside him on either side were the twins, Rehan and Farhan Khan. Ever since the twins had found themselves sharing their dorm room with Khalid, the trio had become a common site around the school. It came as no surprise to everyone that they had hit it off so well with Khalid. Being such insipid and weak willed characters themselves, they were only too happy to be led by someone as domineering as Khalid. Khalid looked intently at Yusif, with a rather forced smile across his face.

"That was a very, er...good recitation you did back there!" he said, searching for his words. There was a tell-tale hint of envy in his voice, and the compliment was clearly a reluctant one. "I was quite surprised..." he continued.

"*Jazakallah khairan*, thank you," replied Yusif politely.

Khalid had always been rather pleased with the fact the he was the only boy in the year who had travelled quite widely around the Muslim world. He felt that it made him one level above the rest of his peers. As he looked at Yusif, he began to wonder whether his advantage was under threat from this new boy.

"Did you study abroad – who was your teacher?" asked Khalid sharply. Yusif was taken aback by the directness of his tone, and was puzzled by Khalid's apparent agitation.

"No! I had a real excellent Ustad back home, *mashallah*. He studied in Syria – where he's from, I think."

"Why, what's it to you?" asked Reda rudely.

"Nothing – I just wondered that's all," replied Khalid, forcing a smile on to his face again.

"I was taught by teachers abroad. When my parents were studying at the Al-Azhar University in Cairo, they were able to find me tutors from the university as well," boasted Khalid. He turned to look at Yusif. At this, Reda gave a loud yawn, and glanced over his shoulder, with his eyebrows arching upwards. He had heard this a hundred times before, and was thoroughly unimpressed by Khalid's conceited manner. Yusif frowned back at Reda, clearly objecting to the rather harsh response of his friend.

"Actually, I was thinking that when I become year captain, you could help me set up a *tajweed* club after school," suggested Khalid.

"Hang on – " interrupted Reda. "What makes you so certain *you'll* be the year captain?"

"Well, I *am* one of the best in our year – don't you think?" boasted Khalid unashamedly. He turned to look at the twins for support. They stood sniggering to each other.

"Absolutely, I can't think of anyone better, can you Farhan?" asked Rehan to his sibling.

"Nope – I'm definitely voting for you Khalid!" replied Farhan. Khalid smiled confidently.

However, the truth of it was that Khalid felt anything but confident inside. His house, Ibn Majah had proved to be a huge disappointment. This was largely because of the 'dimwits' as he considered them, that made up the house. So far, they were behind Ibn Kathir in points. Reda's essay on Imam Al Nawawi's life had scored top marks and that had started his house off on a good footing. This had been a double blow for Khalid, who was quite convinced that his own essay about his trip along the Nile would have seen him to the top of the class for that particular assignment. And it did not stop there! For in the weeks that followed, Ibn Kathir had continued to amass points.

Before the term had even begun, Khalid had

been particularly eager to start back at school. This was going to be the first year where students would have the opportunity to actually make a difference in the school. As year captain he could get to sit on the student council, and work with the year captains of other years on school activities. He would have the ear of the head boy and maybe even the headmaster himself.

Sadly for Khalid, his dreams of succeeding to become year captain were fast disappearing. At the rate Ibn Majah House was going, there was slim chance of them winning and him being nominated! And now, the arrival of the 'new boy' Yusif, with his splendid Qur'an recitation had added to his insecurities. This new boy was proving to be very popular amongst the other boys in the year. Khalid realised that if Ibn Kathir House was to win the house competition, then Yusif himself stood a good chance of being selected. All these thoughts bothered him, as he now stood before his new rival.

"Well, nobody else seems to be interested in the job so far, *do they?*" Khalid asked, studying Yusif's face very carefully as he accentuated the last words. Yusif stared back at Khalid uncomfortably. He *is* rather annoying, thought Yusif to himself. In a way, he could understand why Reda, Warsoma and Daud were eager for him to stand for year captain. The thought of Khalid doing the job was just awful! Nonetheless, Yusif was not completely convinced that he was suitable for the job himself. The thought was just too terrifying!

"Oh, I'm sure there'll be plenty of candidates by the end of the year!" replied Yusif. He hoped that might draw the attention of Reda, Warsoma and Daud away from him. After all, they could still pin their hopes on someone else, *anyone* but him.

Khalid however was none too pleased with Yusif's answer. The four friends took their leave and walked away towards the canteen for lunch. Khalid was left behind at the fountain in a very thoughtful mood. As he wondered how to get Ibn Majah into pole position, his eyes unconsciously fell on a figure scurrying across the courtyard towards the Ibn Majah dorm. On closer inspection, he recognised his friend Saqib Khan.

Khalid had first met Saqib in the Ibn Majah common room. If anyone knew all there was to know about the school, it was Saqib. He was full of stories and tales about the school, its history and its buildings. He had learnt all about how the school had been founded, and even boasted about having knowledge of secret passages that had remained undiscovered for decades.

Suddenly, the corners of Khalid's lips curled, as a sly smile appeared across his face. A thought had struck him, and he was clearly quite pleased about it. Rehan recognised the look immediately.

"What is it Khalid, what are you thinking?" he asked.

"I think I know what to do to make sure Ibn Majah House wins!" replied Khalid.

"How? That's..." began Rehan.

"...impossible isn't it?" finished Farhan.

"C'mon I have to speak to Saqib – he may have the answer to our little problem!"

With this, the three boys hurried towards the dorms of Ibn Majah.

Chapter Nine

Abdul Kadir

"Daud, how long are you going to take in there? Can you hurry up please?" screamed Reda as he stood outside the bathroom with his towel tossed carelessly over his shoulders. Yusif was busy packing his bag in preparation for the year seven science field trip. The boys were travelling with Ustad Zakariya to Hastings beach to make a study of sea life, as part of their term project.

"You should've got up sooner!" said Yusif as he packed his sketchbook, wax crayons and coloured pencils into his rucksack.

"Well it's not my fault I couldn't sleep last night," retorted Reda. "Not with all the commotion coming from next door?"

"What do you mean?" asked Warsoma, who was busy rummaging through his desk, looking for a copy of the *Sea Life Encyclopaedia*. "I didn't hear anything!"

"Well of course you wouldn't," said Reda, "you could sleep through a storm! I don't know what was going on, but there certainly was a lot of tapping coming from there last night. I hardly got a wink of sleep!"

"That's strange," said Warsoma continuing his

search. "Did anyone move my *Sea Life Encyclopaedia*, it's not in my drawer?" By then, Reda had moved away from the bathroom door to stand in front of the mirror. Not paying any attention to Warsoma, he had far more important things on his mind. He was busy scrutinising his reflection, when suddenly his mood brightened.

After getting no response to his question, Warsoma looked up from his desk and started to grin, as he watched Reda's close scrutiny of himself in the mirror. "Don't worry *akhi*, you're still the fairest of them all!" said Warsoma cheekily.

"Eh? No, look! I think I have a hair on my chin – see!" responded Reda proudly. Warsoma jumped to his feet to take a closer look.

"Where, let me see?" He grabbed Reda's chin and tilted it up towards the light.

"Nah...it's just a bit of fluff!" laughed Warsoma, slapping his friend lightly across his cheeks.

Reda looked again, carefully stroking his chin. "You're just jealous!" replied Reda indignantly. "You watch, I'll soon have a beard, *inshallah.*" He gestured with his hand, closed into a tight fist held under his chin. The boys shook their heads as they laughed at him.

"Well I'm ready and packed!" said Yusif. "I just need to run down to the library to get an encyclopaedia for myself."

"Don't you have your own copy?" asked Warsoma.

"I do, but I left my copy behind at home when I went back over the holidays," came the reply.

"I thought I'd do some reading in preparation. But I didn't get the chance in the end. My cousin Abdullah stayed over with me the whole time!" said Yusif, recalling his visit back to Birmingham for the winter break. It had been a lot of fun seeing his family and old friends. Furthermore, he discovered that he was finally going to have a little brother or sister for company. Ammi was expecting a baby!

In fact, Ammi had missed Yusif so much while he was away at boarding school, that to have him home for the holidays came as a great relief to her. As soon as she had laid eyes upon her darling son, the tears had begun to well up in her eyes.

"*Oh, Yusif!*" she exclaimed, shaking her head. "What have they done to you? Didn't they feed you? I'm sure you've lost weight!" She pinched his cheeks and was devastated to have found them 'not so full as they used to be'.

Of course, he hadn't lost any weight at all! He had simply had a 'growth spurt', as Abu correctly observed, noting that he was a full inch taller than when they had last met.

Nonetheless, Ammi still proceeded to spend the next two weeks almost continuously feeding him.

"You won't get chicken biryani like this when you're back in Hastings, you know!" she would say. It seemed as though no sooner had they arrived, than the holidays were over. Once again, Yusif was packing up his cases for the long journey back. He smiled as he recalled his mother's parting words.

"Mark my words, you'll forget something!"

she had warned, as she folded up his neatly pressed pyjamas. She was right. He had been so relaxed about the packing, that it was inevitable that he would leave *something* behind. And so it was, that he was delivered safely back to the Dar Al Ilm Academy – one notch looser on his belt strap, but no *Sea Life Encyclopaedia!*

"It shouldn't take me long at the library," said Yusif as he hastened out of the door. He turned to look over his shoulder at his roommates.

"I'll meet you all in the courtyard," he called, "and you'd better hurry up or we'll miss the coach!"

After he had left the room, he heard Warsoma whoop with relief as he found his missing encyclopaedia, tucked away on the bookshelf.

"That's so strange," he mused. "I could have sworn I left it on my desk!"

Yusif hurried to the library and as he had expected for that time in the morning, it was not busy. The Dar Al Ilm library was a glorious maze of bookcases, filled with volumes both new and old. As he walked through the aisles, he ran his fingers over the rows of books, sniffing the air. He loved the fusion of scents from the rosewood bookcases and the old leather bindings. After a good five minutes sifting through the 'Natural Sciences' section, he had found what he needed and was soon on his way towards the agreed rendezvous point.

It was a chilly morning in January, and a light mist hung in the air. Watching his condensed breath evaporate in front of his face, Yusif hoped that the weather would improve before they got to the beach. He sighed at the thought of traipsing through wet sand

and rummaging around in rock pools using fingers numb with cold. He had been eagerly looking forward to his first school outing ever since it was announced at the end of the last term. He did not want anything to spoil it.

As he stood outside the old iron door that led to his dorms, his eyes focused once again on the inscription engraved on the wooden plaque above it. He had read the inscription so many times now that it was committed to his memory. But no matter how many times he saw them, he just could not decipher the meaning behind the words:

'Live for this life as though you will live forever, and live for your hereafter as though you would die tomorrow.'

[Imam Ali]

Yusif stood with his head tilted to the side, pondering over its meaning.

"*Assalamu alaikum* Yusif – it is Yusif isn't it?" said a cheerful voice from behind him. It was Abdul Kadir the head boy, who happened to be passing by. He had been awake late into the night, studying for his exams, and was on his way to the canteen for a well-deserved breakfast.

"I hope it's not termites you've found?" he laughed as he followed Yusif's gaze towards the door frame. Yusif looked round a little surprised, and slightly nervous.

"Yes, it is Yusif..." he replied shyly, "and no – no I haven't seen any termites!"

"Good! Sheikh Ansari wouldn't be pleased to hear it if there were any!" smiled Abdul Kadir, as he proceeded to explain how the headmaster had noted that far too much money was going towards the restoration work at the school.

"So what's so interesting about the door then?" he asked.

"Oh, nothing! It's just the inscription above it. I don't understand what it means..." replied Yusif gesturing his hand towards the plaque above the door. Abdul Kadir read the words out aloud,

"Live for this life as though you will live forever, and live for your hereafter as though you would die tomorrow."

He stood very thoughtful for a moment, crossing his arms as he contemplated its meaning.

"Well, my young brother, these are the beautiful words of wisdom from the Prophet Muhammad's cousin, Imam Ali ibn Abu Talib," explained Abdul Kadir.

"But it says to live this life as though you will live forever. But we don't live forever, so why live it that way?" quizzed Yusif.

"Exactly!" replied Abdul Kadir. "You see, Imam Ali was talking about the purpose of life for Muslims, and worshiping Allah, as it is described in the Qur'an. He was reminding us of the importance of working for the afterlife – the *akhirah*, as death can come at any time."

Yusif looked up at the words, still a little confused. Abdul Kadir continued to explain how people

could often be so tied up in their day-to-day lives, that they could forget why Allah had created them in the first place. But Abdul Kadir sensed Yusif was still puzzled.

"Let me put it this way, Yusif," he said. "If you had something to do and had all the time in the world to do it, would you be in a hurry?"

"Well, no! Not if I thought I had lots of time!" said Yusif, without hesitation.

"And if you had something really important to do and knew you would die tomorrow, what then?" continued the head boy.

"Then I would hurry up and do it...*Ahhh*!" Yusif gasped, as he finally understood the full meaning.

"Live 'for this life' means worldly ambitions – which you can afford to take your time with," he suggested. "Instead, you should make yourself busy with things that will help you in the *akhirah*, as if you would die tomorrow, and haven't got much time to do them."

"Precisely!" said Abdul Kadir, throwing his arms in the air with satisfaction. "The actions which will help you in the next life are more worthy of focussing your efforts upon."

Yusif smiled. They really were beautiful words of wisdom!

"So little *akhi*, how is your time passing here at Dar Al Ilm Academy?" enquired Abdul Kadir on a different note.

"I like it here – it's going really well, I guess!" replied Yusif.

"You guess? You don't sound very sure. You're not

having problems in class are you, or with friends...?" Abdul Kadir looked suddenly a little concerned.

"No, class is good," replied Yusif eagerly. "And I've made lots of friends. It's just that..." Yusif paused, wondering whether he should say anything further.

After all, Abdul Kadir seemed nice but Yusif didn't really know him. Everything *was* fine at school, but he was still troubled by what the boys had been discussing at the end of last term. Reda, Warsoma and Daud had not approached the subject of year captain with him since then. But Yusif was feeling guilty that they were disappointed with him, especially Reda. They had not said anything, but he had *sensed* it. Maybe Abdul Kadir could help now – after all, he was head boy. Yusif looked at the senior pupil thoughtfully for a moment, and then his mind was made up!

"I had a disagreement with my friends. They think I should stand for year captain and I don't want to!" said Yusif quickly, before he had time to lose his courage. He had to speak to someone to ask for advice, and Abdul Kadir seemed nice and might understand.

Abdul Kadir suddenly relaxed as he realised Yusif's predicament. His features softened, full of sympathy.

"Ah, I see! And may I ask why you don't wish to stand?" asked Abdul Kadir.

Yusif looked a bit uncomfortable. Pulling at his collar, he swallowed the knot that had formed in his throat.

"I just don't think I could do it. I...I wouldn't know what to do!" he stammered. But even as he said the words, they sounded like very feeble excuses.

Abdul Kadir continued to look on kindly at the young boy. Yusif would have been surprised if he had known what Abdul Kadir was thinking. For Abdul Kadir himself had been in just the same position last year when he had been asked to become head boy. He too had been confused and worried, just like Yusif. He paused for a moment, and chose his words carefully.

"You know, when you try to do something new it's natural to feel a little daunted. I was very nervous when I was made head boy," admitted Abdul Kadir.

Yusif was surprised at what he was hearing. Never in his wildest expectations did he think that someone like Abdul Kadir would have felt like that.

"Really? I can't believe it!" gasped Yusif.

"It's true!" assured Abdul Kadir. "I didn't want to be nominated, and I didn't even put myself forward for the task, but in the end I still got chosen!" replied Abdul Kadir, earnestly. He recalled his feelings – how shocked he had been when his name came up in the nominations, and how reluctant he had been at the thought of accepting the position. It was one of the hardest decisions he had faced in his life.

He had realised that it was not going to be easy to step into the shoes of the head boy. Not only would he have the pressure of working for his final exams, but he would also have to bear his responsibilities towards the welfare of the school community. It was a tall order, even for the most able of pupils.

"So what changed your mind?" asked Yusif, hoping that he may find some answers for his own dilemma.

Abdul Kadir smiled.

"It was simple. I was told that it could be a great source of reward," he replied. "A person who was very dear to me also pointed out that it was the right thing to do. It is a Muslim's duty to be concerned about the welfare of his community and to help others – to be there for them. Like that saying of Imam Ali above the door, it's living for *akhirah*," he continued. "Sometimes you have to be prepared to overcome personal difficulties if it means that it would be doing the right thing by Islam."

Seeing Yusif still a little apprehensive, he thought for a moment about another way to encourage him. He looked up and caught sight of the inscribed words again.

"Look at Imam Ali himself as an example," said the head boy. "He was only a few years younger than you when he had to make a huge decision. The Prophet, peace be upon him, invited him to Islam. Do you know what his response was?"

Yusif thought carefully, racking his brains to find the answer.

"No!" he replied finally, as he realised that he was not familiar with the story.

"Well, he said that he would have to ask his father's permission first. But later he realised that Allah had not asked his father's permission before he created him, so no matter how difficult it would be, or what opposition he might face, he decided that he should accept the invitation, because he knew Islam was the truth. It was a great test for him, and he stepped up to the mark. These are but tests of life that we are given by Allah, even for those as young as you."

Yusif listened thoughtfully. He had not considered his predicament in that way before. Admittedly, Abdul Kadir's words made sense. Yusif sighed heavily.

"Think about it carefully – don't be too quick to dismiss it!" smiled Abdul Kadir, tapping Yusif's back with encouragement. Yusif smiled and promised that he *would* think about it.

At that moment, the old iron door opened. Reda, Warsoma and Daud emerged with their rucksacks on their backs, all ready to head off on the day's excursion.

"Yusif ! Oh – *assalamu alaikum* brother Abdul Kadir!" said Warsoma with a start, as he noticed the head boy standing in front of him.

"*Wa alaikum assalaam* Warsoma, boys," replied Abdul Kadir, looking curiously at their bags. "You look like you're about to make a great escape with those packs on your backs!" he teased. "Are you going somewhere nice?"

"We've got our year seven field trip to Hastings beach today," replied Reda. "The coach leaves at nine." Abdul Kadir looked at his watch. It had just turned nine, and raising his eyebrows, he looked at the boys with concern.

"Shouldn't you all be at the entrance hall by now?" he asked.

"Yes, but Daud made us late!" teased Reda, looking back at the guilty culprit. Poor Daud – his cheeks flushed bright red.

"Go on – you'd best hurry," advised Abdul Kadir.

"Otherwise Ustad Zakariya will have you on litter duty for delaying everyone." With this, the boys gave their *salams* and quickly made their way to the entrance hall.

Ustad Zakariya was waiting anxiously, looking at the clock. Dressed in green Wellington boots and a raincoat, he looked ready to brave the harshest elements that Hastings beach could muster. Reda grinned as he looked at the teacher's apparel. But his humour was short lived, as he noted the grim expression upon Ustad Zakariya's face.

"Well boys, there had better be good reason for your tardiness!" boomed Ustad Zakariya. Reda gulped nervously.

Chapter Ten

Sand, Sea, Pebbles and Life

Yusif drew his breath in slowly, as he took in the freshness of the salty sea air around him. The waters of the Hastings beach were a breathtaking vision of azure. White frothy waves rolled gently back and forth over the pebbles along the shoreline. Seagulls circled high in the sky above, cawing with their familiar sound that seemed to echo all around the beach. Despite the season, it was a crisp and sunny morning. Yusif gazed on in wonder. It had been years since he had last seen the sea. He marvelled at the beautiful scene before him, and contemplated the majesty and the artistry of Allah.

And to think, he could have missed all of this if he and the boys had not been able to convince Ustad Zakariya to let them on the coach after their late arrival! After profuse apologies from the four of them, Ustad Zakariya had relented and decided to overlook their tardiness *this time*.

"If it ever happens again..." he had warned the boys and the rest of the class, "I can assure you that you will be left behind at school without a second thought."

Judging from the stern look on his face, they could tell that he meant every word. After all, punctuality was one of Ustad Zakariya's key requirements from his pupils. He had often reminded them, that it is a mark of good character for a Muslim to keep to their appointments.

The journey was quite a short one. Twenty minutes was all it took to reach Hastings beach. In fact, the Academy was not at all far from the beach, but the road links were quite circuitous, and made the journey seem much longer. Ustad Ibrahim and Ustad O'Malley had also been enlisted to supervise on the day of the field trip, and they accompanied the boys on the coach.

On the beach, Ustad Zakariya gave a brief address about the 'dos and do nots' of the day. The gathered boys listened eagerly, itching to begin their explorations.

"Rule number one..." he announced. "There will be *definitely* no swimming in the sea." This news sent a wave of painful moans along the shoreline. Despite the cold, many of the boys had been hoping for a quick dip, particularly Reda, who had worn his long swimming trunks underneath his trousers in anticipation. The Ustad continued.

"There will be no rock climbing, no wandering off on your own, no sand fights, and *absolutely* no tasting anything you might consider to be edible..." Yusif cringed at the thought.

"...and by the way, no seaweed is to be slipped down the backs of your classmates! Is that clear?"

"Boo!" cried some of the boys. Others broke into laughter. Warsoma sighed in relief, knowing that he was all too often the target of Reda's practical jokes.

"*Alhamdulillah*! I knew we'd all agree!" smiled Ustad Zakariya, his eyes twinkling at the sight of the keen young faces before him. He reminded the boys of their assignments, which had been discussed in class the day before.

"*Khalas* – off you go!" he exclaimed, as he raised his hands and dismissed the boys. He looked on as they clambered off in different directions.

The boys had been split into teams. Yusif, Warsoma, Reda, Daud, Azmi, Hamudi and Harun were together in one group. Their mission was to locate the items on a list of 'sea life and fauna', to examine them and to make sketches. They then had to produce a sketch of a typical rock pool, categorising its contents into plants and sea creatures. Lastly, each boy had to collect one item of particular interest. The best object would win five points for the respective house.

Before long, Yusif was wandering up and down the beach with his fellow team members, hunting carefully for rock pools or any interesting sea life. He had gathered a few things in his bucket, when he spotted a patch of golden sand amongst the pebbles near the shoreline. He decided to leave his friends to explore it. With a sudden urge to feel the sand on his feet, he took off his socks and boots and walked along the sandy tract. Swimming had been banned, but Yusif figured that this was the next best thing.

The sight of the sea, which shimmered as it met the horizon in the far distance, captivated his attention.

Suddenly, he gasped as an icy chill moved through his limbs and diverted his focus for a moment. Looking down he realised that he had stopped and sunk deep into the sand. The cold water gushed around his ankles, as the tide gently rolled in. Yusif wriggled his toes as the water receded, and laughed to himself as the shifting sand tickled the soles of his bare feet.

He looked down at the bucket he was holding in his hands and admired his collection. It contained a number of weird and wonderful specimens. So far, he had found a blue-rayed limpet, a cowrie (which was a small seed shaped shell, whose surface was rough and grooved), some dogwhelk, and a pair of mussels.

"Ahoy there Yusif, we need the fish net!" cried Reda from a short distance away. Turning his attention away from the bucket, Yusif looked over his shoulder towards the boys. They were stood near some rocks, waving and shouting frantically. So much enthusiasm could only mean one thing – they had found a suitable rock pool.

Yusif had been delegated the responsibility of holding the fishing net. After quickly putting his footwear back on, he dashed across the pebbled beach towards the others, his cheeks flushed from the cool sea breeze.

"Sorry *akhi*, here you go," said Yusif as he handed over the net. He dropped down to his knees beside Reda and Warsoma. The latter was busy reading the chapter on rock pools from his copy of the *Sea Life Encyclopaedia*. He examined the illustrations carefully.

"*Alhamdulillah*, this is more like it!" said Warsoma joyfully.

"There are so many things here!" cried Yusif, staring into the pool of water. "I was beginning to think we wouldn't find a good example."

"Ah! Look there – we found the seaweed we need!" said Warsoma.

"The bubbly brown one is bladderwrack and the red one is corallina. Oh, and that green one over there is... sea lettuce!" he continued.

"Sea lettuce!" exclaimed Reda amused. "Are you going to be putting it into your sandwiches then, Warsoma?"

"I'll put it in *your* sandwiches, if you like!" responded Warsoma, as he continued to finger through the encyclopaedia.

At this point, Azmi interjected, unable to resist the urge to point out rule number five.

"Don't forget what Ustad Zakariya told us – no eating your specimens!" he said, grinning broadly. With this, his attention was suddenly diverted. He noticed something that looked like a small rock peeping out from beneath some fronds of the bladderwrack.

"Look guys, what's that over there?" he asked, pointing into the water. "Move over *akhi*, it might make a good addition to our collection."

Azmi squeezed himself between Daud and Yusif. He rolled up his sleeves and stuck his hand into the pool of water. He grimaced as his fingers curled around the slippery seaweed that began to tangle itself around his hands.

"Here, put it in my bucket!" offered Yusif, pushing the bucket towards Azmi.

"*Foo yo*, this seaweed is so slimy!" said Azmi, gratefully depositing it in the bucket.

"That's much better, I can see it now," he declared, satisfied at having cleared the area for a closer inspection. He put his hand back in the water, whilst the boys gathered around him watching eagerly.

Azmi gently pushed a small rock aside. He looked closely. Suddenly, he gave out a loud yelp, which made Yusif and Warsoma jump to their feet in fright.

"*Ya Allah!*" cried Harun, yanking Azmi's wrist out of the water.

"What happened? Is it a jellyfish, are you stung?" asked Harun, frantically turning Azmi's hands over. Azmi shook his head.

"No, I...I felt something move and it felt weird..." he stuttered, shuddering as he recalled the feeling.

"Don't be ridiculous, Harun," exclaimed Warsoma. "You can't find jellyfish in rock pools...erm, I think!"

Then Reda, who was at this point the only one still standing beside the rock pool, burst into laughter as he peered into the water. Grabbing the end of the fish net, he plunged it into the water and gently moved the rock aside again.

"*Ya akhi* – it's just a starfish, see!" he said. The boys edged forward, slowly surrounding the rock pool once again. Reda scooped the starfish gently up in his

hand and lifted it out of the water. It was a curiously shaped but perfectly formed creature. Azmi looked at it cautiously.

"Azmi, come closer," invited Reda. "Do you want to hold it?"

"No fear!" exclaimed Azmi clearly perturbed by the idea of touching the creature. "Erm, I mean it's okay, I can see perfectly well from here, and I don't need to hold it," he continued, half expecting it to jump out of Reda's hand and latch on to his face with its suckers. It would no doubt be an act of vengeance for having disturbed its peaceful abode in such a fashion.

Reda grinned mischievously.

"Stop teasing him!" said Yusif. "Here, let me hold it!"

Reda placed his hand above Yusif's and with a slight twist, dropped the creature gently into Yusif's palm.

"What's it called?" asked Yusif turning to look at Warsoma, who began to rifle through the pages of his *Sea Life Encyclopaedia*.

"I think it's a...erm, cushion star?" replied Warsoma shrugging his shoulders. Identifying the little sea creature proved not to be as easy as Warsoma had anticipated.

Yusif stroked it with his little finger and watched with curiosity as its five arms curled in response to his touch. Its body was soft and slimy, with brown speckles.

"What was all that screaming about?" boomed

a voice from behind the rocks. A little startled, Yusif looked up to see the familiar figure of Ustad Ibrahim heading towards them. He had been walking nearby when the commotion by the rock pool had erupted, and felt it was his duty to investigate what was going on. As he stood looking now at the boys, he was relieved to see them safe and sound.

"Azmi went looking for a rock and thought he had found a sea monster!" laughed Reda.

"No I didn't!" retorted Azmi crossly, folding his arms across his chest.

"A *sea monster*, really Reda?" chuckled Ustad Ibrahim.

"I doubt he would be able to find one in a rock pool that size!" Suddenly, he noticed Yusif with his hands carefully held out in front of him.

"Well now, what have you there, Yusif?" asked Ustad Ibrahim. Yusif stretched out his palm, revealing the creature.

"It's a starfish, Ustad," replied Yusif, proud of the catch. "But we don't know what kind exactly!"

Ustad Ibrahim looked at the little creature carefully. He stroked his white beard with his hand, as he always did when he was deep in thought.

"Hmm, I do believe that's a cushion star you have there Yusif!"

"Yes! I knew I was right..." cried Warsoma throwing his fist in the air, evidently somewhat pleased with his earlier identification. Perhaps he was getting the hang of it, after all.

"*Subhanallah*, look at the wonderful creatures that

Allah has created," said Ustad Ibrahim. He gently lifted the starfish from Yusif's hand and placed it in his own. He continued,

"Allah says in the Qur'an,

'*Allah has created every animal from water. Of them are some that creep on their bellies, some that walk on two legs, and some that walk on four. Allah creates what He wills, for truly Allah has power over all things.*'"

The boys crowded around Ustad Ibrahim, listening intently. They stared at the starfish again, this time with a renewed curiosity.

"Did you know boys, a cushion starfish starts life as a male and at about four years old, it turns into a female," explained Ustad Ibrahim.

"And another thing, imagine that if this cushion star were to loose one of its arms, Allah has given it the ability to grow it back!"

"Wow!" gasped the boys in amazement.

"It's a wonder to me how some people can attribute the existence of such complex creatures, with their sophisticated phases of growth, to be the result of sheer chance," mused Ustad Ibrahim.

"My grandfather believes that," said Daud quietly. "He's an athi – " But he was unable to finish his sentence, as he struggled to pronounce his last word.

"Do you mean to say he is an atheist?" offered Ustad Ibrahim kindly.

"Yes, that's right! I heard him speaking to my father once. He did his best to convince my grandfather about the existence of Allah, but he wouldn't believe it. He says we all came from a bowl of soup, which

I thought was strange!" sighed Daud.

The boys laughed at Daud's description. Yusif smiled to himself as he contemplated the vision of Daud's grandfather springing out of a tin of minestrone. Ustad Ibrahim coughed discreetly, directing a gentle look of disapproval at the gathered boys.

"I think your grandfather was referring to the theory of the *primordial* soup, Daud," explained Ustad Ibrahim. The boys looked at each other blankly. Ustad Ibrahim realised that further elaboration was needed.

"You see, some people do not believe there is a God, but that life began in the oceans. They propose that as a result of a combination of chemicals in the atmosphere, the building blocks of life were formed, which went on to evolve into all of the species."

"That doesn't make sense to me, Ustad!" said Daud shaking his head in disagreement. "Where then did they think the oceans and the atmosphere came from?" asked Daud with a puzzled expression across his face. Ustad Ibrahim smiled.

"Precisely – what created the atmosphere and the oceans in the first place?" questioned Ustad Ibrahim. "And what brought about the right chemical conditions to form life? These questions remain unanswered by their theory. It is nothing but conjecture."

Ustad Ibrahim paused. He took his eyes off the starfish for a moment to look across at the great expanse of the sea. It was much calmer now compared to when they had arrived earlier in the morning. He was no stranger to this landscape. He would often go there at dawn, just as the sun began to rise. Its brilliant reflection would shimmer on the surface of the water, tinging the sea with a crimson hue. Never, in all the years that he had visited this beach, did it fail to inspire him and bring him closer to the remembrance of Allah.

"No indeed," he continued, "it is Allah that created the heavens and earth and those that dwell within." He proceeded to quote from the Qur'an once more.

"Verily in the heavens and the earth are signs for those who believe. And in the creation of yourselves, and the fact that animals are scattered (through the earth), are signs for those of assured faith. And in the alternation of night and day, and the fact that Allah sends down sustenance from the sky, and revives therewith the earth after its death, and in the change of the winds, are signs for those who are wise..."

"You see boys, Islam teaches us that human beings are a unique form of life that was created by Allah in a special way, with special gifts and abilities that were not given to other creatures," said Ustad Ibrahim.

"What do you mean by gifts, Ustad?" asked Reda.

"Well, Allah gave us a soul, a conscience, knowledge, and free will," explained Ustad Ibrahim. "This is what sets us apart from the other things He created. So as Muslims, we do not believe that human beings randomly evolved from some chemical reaction. The life of human beings began when Allah created the first two people, a man and a woman named Adam and Eve. And one of the signs of Allah's involvement is the various races and languages

He created. You have only to look at each other to appreciate this fact."

The boys glanced curiously at each other. It was as though they were seeing one another for the first time, from a new perspective. They noticed the differences in their own features, each from distinct races and with varied languages, yet all brothers in Islam.

Ustad Ibrahim knelt down and lowered his hand gently into the rock pool, returning the cushion star to its home. He watched as the starfish re-attached itself to the rock.

The boys were amazed to see how perfectly it camouflaged itself within its natural habitat. The colour of the little creature matched the rock, hue for hue. What a wondrous creation it was, full of purpose and design! They marvelled at the intricacy of Allah's creation.

"Such complexity as seen in life forms, the immense order we observe in the universe and the laws that govern it cannot come about by random chance!" concluded Ustad Ibrahim, as he watched the starfish blend away and virtually disappear against its rocky background.

"There, back where it belongs. Now boys, don't forget to draw a diagram of it in your sketch books!" advised Ustad Ibrahim.

"Yes, Sir!" replied the boys in unison.

Ustad Ibrahim smiled at Azmi, who was looking on in a kind of silent sulk.

"I'm not surprised you had a shock Azmi," said Ustad Ibrahim sympathetically. "I would never have seen it on the rock surface myself." Fortunately, his words had the desired effect. Azmi brightened up a little, his lips curling ever so slightly into a smile.

"Well boys, you had better finish your work quickly," said Ustad Ibrahim glancing down at his watch. We only have about an hour and a half left before we..." He stopped mid-sentence, as his eyes looked up towards the cliffs not far from where they were standing.

"You boys there! Khalid, Rehan and Farhan!" he shouted. "What are you doing over there?"

Yusif and the boys turned to look at the cliffs. Almost like mountains, they towered menacingly over the beach. Their weathered rocks were jagged and white, as though covered in ice and snow. Khalid and the twins looked small and fragile beside them. The trio appeared to be so engrossed in examining the cliffs that they had not noticed how treacherously narrow the beach was in that area. From there, the three of them ran the risk of being cut off from the main beach if the tide suddenly swept in. It was no wonder that Ustad Ibrahim seemed worried about them. With this, Ustad Ibrahim hurried off leaving the boys behind by the rock pool.

"What are they up to, I wonder?" said Yusif, his brow frowning.

"Not anything good by the looks of it," replied Reda as he stood watching curiously with folded arms.

"Oh! Who cares?" cried Warsoma in frustration, now sitting cross-legged on the rocks and staring into the pool.

"C'mon you guys, let's finish here and get going. We still have to find our individual objects remember?" With his sketchbook wide open on his lap and coloured pencils beside him, he began frantically sketching the outline of the rock pool. Heeding his warnings the other boys soon joined him as they settled down to do the same.

Chapter Eleven

Show and Tell

"Is that all you could find on the beach?" asked Ustad Zakariya incredulously, looking at an old boot as it hung from the tatty shoestring clenched between Zulfi's fingers. Zulfi smiled and nodded his head.

"Yes, but this is no *ordinary* boot, Sir," insisted Zulfi. "It's a boot that came all the way across the channel from France!"

"Hmm, and you think that makes it interesting?" laughed Ustad Zakariya. In all his years of teaching, this had to be one of the most unusual souvenirs to have been brought back from Hastings beach.

It had been almost a week ago that the boys of year seven had been exploring the beach. They were now sitting in class ready to display their findings for all to see. Yusif, Warsoma, Daud and Reda sat silent and downcast, while the rest of their classmates were busy giggling over Zulfi's offering.

The classroom laughter seemed to fade into the background, as Yusif pondered to himself over the events of that morning. All thoughts of the present commotion in the class were placed on hold, as he remembered what had happened...

He had awoken in the morning to the sound of

knocking and banging in the dorm room. He propped himself up on one arm to look out over his bunk, when a strange feeling of déjà vu came over him. He was startled at the sight of Warsoma rummaging through his drawers. The whole place was a mess. It was as though a hurricane had swept through their room!

"What's the matter Warsoma?" asked Yusif.

"I can't find my sketch book *akhi*, have you seen it?" asked Warsoma, as he lunged forward attacking the bookshelf, emptying it of its contents one by one.

"No, but did you check your rucksack?" replied Yusif, slowly descending the ladder of his bunk bed.

"I checked there first. I haven't looked at it since the day of the school trip – I don't understand, I've searched everywhere!" moaned Warsoma as he sunk to the floor, staring at the piles of books around him. He was holding his face in his hands. His head shook from side to side, as he racked his brains wondering where it could have gone.

Suddenly, a look of dread swept over him as he turned to look at Yusif.

"What if I've left it back at the beach?" he cried. "Look at this place, I've turned it upside down – it's not here! What will Ustad Zakariya say? My rock pool project is ruined!"

'Poor Warsoma', thought Yusif to himself.

"*Assalamu alaikum akhi* – what's happening?" yawned Daud as he got up from his slumber. Reda too began to stir with the noise of the voices in the room.

"Wow! What happened to the room?" exclaimed Reda as he hung over his bunk and jumped effortlessly down.

Yusif explained about the missing sketchbook, as it was evident, that by now, Warsoma was far too upset to speak.

"Maybe we should all check our own bags in case one of us picked it up," suggested Daud. The three boys got their rucksacks out, but the book was nowhere to be seen.

"What about the shell you found. Do you *at least* have that for 'show and tell'?" asked Reda.

Warsoma sniffed his nose, holding back the tears. He nodded his head.

"Well, that's something – don't worry I'm sure Ustad Zakariya will understand. It's Allah's will that the book got left behind," said Daud trying his best to console Warsoma. Suddenly there was a loud gasp from Yusif's direction.

"Hey! The old coins I found at the beach are missing!" exclaimed Yusif, as he sifted frantically through his rucksack.

"Didn't you give them to Ustad Zakariya?" asked Daud, "I thought he was going to hand the coins over to the authorities?"

"No! He said I could keep them till the end of today's lesson, where we present our objects for 'show and tell', remember?" replied Yusif. "But after that I would have to give them over to him. They must have fallen out of my bag, I guess," said Yusif with a very disappointed tone in his voice. He had been looking forward to presenting them to the class, especially as Ustad Zakariya had seemed so excited about the find...

A loud guffaw from one of his classmates suddenly brought Yusif back to the present moment. He looked closely at the glass jar he held in his hands. On the day at the beach, Yusif had managed to find some other souvenirs as well as the coins, one of which was a sponge that washed up on the shoreline. He had brought it to class inside the jar. Having read about the sponge in Warsoma's *Sea Life Encyclopaedia*, he was surprised to discover that it was an animal and not a plant. It was creamy white, and its body was covered with pores. As the sea water flowed through these tiny holes, the sponge would filter out food. It was these same pores, Yusif had learnt, that made the object a useful bathtime accessory.

Poor Yusif had tried to convince himself that it was a suitable alternative to his missing coins. But as he prepared the speech in his head, he knew in his heart that it was not a *unique* find – not like two ancient coins of a bygone era.

* * *

It was in fact just after he had picked up the sponge that Yusif had found them. He had wandered into a remote pebbly area of the beach, and while he was pulling it out from between the stones, he had noticed a glint on the ground in front. On closer inspection, he saw the two circular metallic objects.

Initially, he had thought they were just loose change that someone had inadvertently dropped.

However, when he picked them up, he realised there was something most peculiar about them. For a start, they were not neatly circular, but had irregular edges. And unlike modern money, they had a picture of a man with curly hair and what looked like a wreath on his head. He had taken the coins to Ustad Zakariya, who had confirmed that the head was most likely that of a Roman emperor. Yusif had found coins from well over a thousand years ago!

But now the coins were missing, and Yusif only had the sponge to offer. Two other boys, Sufyan Hamdi and Muhammad Diwan had both found sponges as well, but fortunately for him they were not in class 7b! The coins on the other hand, were a real find. No one else in their year, or any other year for that matter, had ever found anything like them. That was what Ustad Zakariya had said on the day at the beach.

"You don't often see anything like this Yusif – well done!" he had exclaimed, as he examined one of the little coins. Holding it in the air, he turned it carefully between his fingers. They were bronze coloured pieces of flat metal that shimmered a little in the light of the midday sun. But they were so old, scratched and battered that it made it difficult to place their age. Ustad Zakariya had explained that the stormy waves of the night before must have washed them up onto the shore. Apparently, that was the best time to find treasures on the beach.

* * *

Yusif let out a faint sigh as he remembered his little treasure. His turn had arrived to speak to the class. Ustad Zakariya looked towards him, his mouth grinning in anticipation.

"Yusif – would you like to talk about your find please?" asked the teacher. Yusif returned from his thoughts with a start.

"Yes, Sir!" he said, as he stood up clutching the jam jar close to him and walked to the front of the class.

"What's this – where are your coins?" asked Ustad Zakariya in surprise. Yusif hung his head.

"I – I lost them!" he stammered. "I think they must have fallen out of my bag at the beach that day."

"*Subhanallah!*" exclaimed the teacher, "It seems like both you *and* Warsoma had a very bad day that day. It's such a pity, your team would have produced one of the best field trip projects otherwise."

This piece of information did not go down very well at all with the boys of Ibn Kathir House. And so, it was with a heavy heart that Yusif proceeded to talk about his sponge.

After the class, lunch was an unusually sombre affair for Yusif and the boys. Yusif, Reda, Warsoma and Daud sat gloomily toying with their food. Normally there would have been laughter and frolics across their table, with the four of them chit-chatting and enjoying their meal. It was Wednesday, and that meant chicken korma was on offer – a great favourite with Yusif and his roommates. Today, however, there was no sign of their usual eagerness. Even raspberry trifle for dessert did not cheer them up. They were sulking at the thought of the valuable points they had lost as a result of their carelessness with their objects.

"What did you all think of Khalid's presentation in 'show and tell'?" asked Reda, staring at the green peas he had separated from the rice, before popping them into his mouth.

"It was very good!" replied Warsoma.

"Yes, it was. He did well finding that ani-mate fossil, don't you think?" remarked Daud.

"You mean *ammonite* fossil," corrected Warsoma. "Yes he did! You don't often see one as well preserved as that. Er, I think..."

"It was really nice to look at," said Yusif as he remembered the object. It was a beautiful specimen of a ribbed, spiral formed shell. It had a glossy surface, and was the colour of black treacle.

"What did he say about it again?"

"They were creatures that lived in the sea about two hundred and fifty million years ago, but they became extinct along with the dinosaurs," answered Warsoma. Just then Azmi and Hamudi joined the table.

"What are you all talking about?" asked Azmi, as he set his tray down opposite to Yusif. The fresh smell of spices diffused in the air, wafting from Azmi's warm plate of chicken korma.

"Khalid's ammonite fossil!" replied Yusif.

"Oh yes, it was an amazing find *laa*," said Azmi. "But nowhere near as good as your old coins, Yusif!" said Azmi.

"We heard Ustad Zakariya talking to Ustad O'Malley after class," added Hamudi. "Even they said your find was the best – and the most rare. You should have got the house points instead of Khalid!"

"Oh no! Did Khalid get the points for Ibn Majah?" asked Reda. Hamudi nodded his head. Having just helped himself to a large spoonful of rice, he gulped it down and took a sip of his juice before continuing.

"It's official, I read it on the notice board. Ibn Majah have overtaken us on the score chart," responded Hamudi. "I mean let's face it – it had to happen! With Yusif's ancient coins gone, all that was left to compare with was limpets, whelks, sponges – oh, and Zulfi's continental boot!"

It was depressingly true, and everyone at the table knew it. Yusif's own emotional state was undergoing a surprising transformation. It bothered him a lot to know that Ibn Kathir House had fallen behind. But why should he care? After all, they were just silly house points – no big deal. But he *did* care. Somewhere deep down inside him, was growing a deep sense of loss. As he pondered over these feelings, the realisation suddenly hit home. '*I do want to be year captain!*' He was upset, and he felt it was unfair that the chance had been taken away from him.

"Where did they find that stupid fossil anyway?" asked Reda highly irritated.

"Most likely the cliffs, that's where you would find them," informed Warsoma as he pushed his plate aside and stuck his spoon into his trifle, trying to separate the layers. First the cream from the custard, then the custard from the raspberry jelly underneath.

"So that's why they went to the cliff side!" exclaimed Yusif.

"Actually, no!" said Azmi dropping his voice to a whisper. He looked over his shoulders to make sure nobody else was listening in.

"I heard something interesting the other day. Some of the boys were saying that Khalid and the twins were looking for smugglers caves!"

"Why? That's not a find," said Warsoma unimpressed as he poked at his jelly. "There's nothing special about them, everyone knows that the Hastings cliffs are riddled with them! Did you know some people even say there are old tunnels under our school building?"

"Maybe they were looking for buried treasure for 'show and tell'," replied Azmi. "I don't know. But that's what they were really doing!"

"What do you mean tunnels under the school?" interrupted Reda, not in the least bit interested by the unlikely thought of buried treasure. But the thought of tunnels under the school – now that did intrigue him. "I've never heard anything about that."

"Oh, it's not true!" laughed Warsoma.

"No, I've heard about them as well," affirmed Hamudi. "Besides it's an old house, why shouldn't there be any? Many old houses have all manner of secret rooms, passages and tunnels. My parents are members of the National Trust, and they're always dragging me around these old places! You know..."

Hamudi stopped short, as he suddenly realised Ustad O'Malley was standing behind him. They had been so engrossed in their discussion, that nobody had seen him strolling towards them. He joined in with their conversation.

"It is true, there was religious unrest during some periods in English history." The other boys looked up, startled at the sight of the teacher.

"There was a steady flow of priests and soldiers needing a place to hide out or a way of making a quick escape," informed Ustad O'Malley.

"That is why a lot of old houses had secret tunnels and passages," he continued.

"But I'm happy to report that the buildings of Dar Al Ilm, whilst very old, are most definitely free from any tunnels!"

"How can you be sure, Ustad?" asked Reda.

"Well, I saw the old plans for the building when they started renovations on the school two years ago," he replied. "The Orangery, the South Wing and the prayer hall were all reconstructed, and there were definitely no drawings of tunnels there," said Ustad O'Malley.

Ustad O'Malley continued to explain that the previous owner of the old mansion had handed the original plans to the school trustees. The house had been in his family for centuries and after he became a Muslim, he had donated the building to the school. If anyone would have known about tunnels, it would have been him. And never did he mention the existence of any hidden tunnels at any time.

"Why are you all so interested to know about tunnels anyway?" asked Ustad O'Malley.

"No reason, Sir! Erm, we were just talking about the smugglers caves by the Hastings cliffs," replied Azmi. "Then someone mentioned about the rumours of there being tunnels under the school."

"Well that's all they are, rumours! Speaking of Hastings beach, that's why I came to talk to you," said Ustad O'Malley, turning his attention towards Yusif. "Ustad Zakariya tells me that you lost the coins!" Yusif nodded his head regretfully.

"Never mind, these things happen – it was Allah's will," he said, realising how disappointed Yusif was about the whole affair. He continued, "But if you should happen to find them, it is very important that you give them to me. We have to report any kind of objects of antiquity to the authorities – coins, jewellery, and things like that. Ah well, such a pity! Never mind, let's hope they will turn up somewhere, *inshallah*."

With this, Ustad O'Malley parted company from the boys with a cheery smile and heartfelt *salams*.

Chapter Twelve

Sabotage!

"*CLEAR!*" shouted Ustad Hamza. The first whistle blew. Yusif's heart was thumping wildly. He slowly drew his arrow back and felt it gently nudge the side of his nose. He pursed his lips as the bowstring lightly pressed against them. The fingers of his left hand were sticky from sweat, but securely gripped his recurve bow. Closing his left eye, he focused straight ahead upon his target, just as Ustad Hamza had taught him. Yusif whispered the *basmala* under his breath, as he paused in anticipation.

A few seconds later, the second whistle blew.

"*FIRE!*" yelled Ustad Hamza at the top of his voice.

In an instant, Yusif's eyes closed. His fingers relaxed around the arrow as it sped away from his grip. He opened his eyes again, his breath held between his lips. He watched anxiously as his arrow tore through the air. Its red tail feathers, the colours of Ibn Kathir, danced and twisted in the breeze.

Yusif was not alone. Eager eyes looked on as the boys of year seven stood motionless in one regimental line across the freshly cut lawn. It was a warm and sunny day for April. Not a sound could be heard, except for the whistle of the arrows cutting through the air as they left their bows and flew across the field. The whistle was closely followed by the whipping sound of the iron arrowheads as they pierced through the woven straw surface of their targets.

After a few seconds a third and final whistle blew.

"*RETRIEVE!*" shouted Ustad Hamza, after checking that all arrows had been fired. "And for those of you who just fired your first arrow, *mabrook*! You have fulfilled the *sunnah* of the Prophet, peace be upon him."

A murmur of excitement broke out with this announcement. Ustad Hamza paused as he smiled and looked along the row of boys before him. They were eager to know how keen their aim had been. Some of them rushed forward to see how they had scored on the target. Others stood rubbing their forearms, which were chafed from the whiplash of the bowstrings. For most of the boys, it was their first effort on the archery field.

Yusif stood rooted to the ground, staring at the target twenty metres ahead. In the weeks that preceded, he had patiently waited for the winter term to pass. With the spring term well under way, the boys had finally been given the news they had been longing to hear. Junior archery classes were to begin. Now, as he stood there on the grass, Yusif could hardly believe that he had finally shot his very first arrow!

"Well done *akhi*, you hit the target!" said Warsoma in awe, who was standing beside him to the left.

"And you're sure you've never done this before?"

he asked somewhat sceptically.

Warsoma raised his hand above his eyes, shading his view from the full glare of the sun, as he peered in wonderment towards Yusif's target.

"Yes, I am sure, Warsoma. Wow, that was amazing!" cried Yusif, almost giddy with excitement.

Meanwhile, Reda was standing to the left of Warsoma, making a lot of noise. He had joined archery club the year before, and was a little more experienced than the others.

"I almost hit the bullseye!" he exclaimed ecstatically, evidently proud of his achievement. "And you *akhi*, did not do so well, as usual!" chortled Reda as he turned towards Warsoma. His hand was gesturing towards Warsoma's arrow, which lay on the ground a few feet in front of them. Warsoma grinned.

"Yes, but you can't deny it's a couple of inches further than last year's attempt!"

"That's true *akhi*. But the arrow is supposed to fly out of the bow, not *fall* out!" said Reda as he slapped Warsoma on his back, laughing heartily as he did so.

"How did you do, Daud?" asked Yusif looking to his right.

Daud was thoughtful. He was staring off far into the distance. He had missed the target altogether, having overshot the mark.

"Well, I thought I was aiming straight. But my arrow went wide. I think I applied too much pressure on the bow..." he said.

Ustad Hamza had warned them about this. He had said that beginners often had a tendency to overstretch the bow in an effort to put more power into the shot.

"But you can be sure your hand will shift the bow over," he had advised. "Then you can say goodbye to your arrow and only pray you won't find it stuck in a tree, or who knows where!"

"Don't worry, Daud," reassured Yusif. "I'm sure you'll get the hang of it! It was still a brilliant first attempt. At least you used the bow and arrow correctly. You just need to work on the aim, that's all!"

The boys walked across the lush, green lawn. Ustad Hamza looked very energised. He was fired up with enthusiasm, and paced briskly towards the row of targets. He was keen to see how the boys had done and then get on to the next round of shots.

"Come on boys! Get your scores checked onto your cards and collect up your arrows, go-go-go lads!" he shouted.

Daud's arrow had lodged into the grass at an angle, a few yards behind his target. Yusif on the other hand, was pleasantly surprised as he stood before his own.

"Not bad for a first attempt!" exclaimed Reda as he pulled his arrow out of the target. "You're well into the target!"

"Oh, it's just beginner's luck!" said Yusif smiling in return. He curled his fingers around his arrow, which was firmly embedded in the red rings of the target, and pulled hard. It really was a decent strike. But it was still nowhere near to the 'X' that marked the bullseye (or 'pinhole' as Reda called it), in the very centre of the ring.

After returning to the shooting line, the boys continued with their target practice for the next couple of hours. With each round, Yusif seemed to generally improve, sometimes missing the target altogether, but once even managing to get quite close to the pinhole. Daud also managed to improve his scores, hitting the target about half of the time. On one shot, he even got the arrow into the gold centre ring – but probably more by accident than skill.

Khalid and the twins were watching their progress with great interest. Khalid stood frowning, as he often did when something upset him – which seemed to Yusif to be most of the time. It was fairly obvious that Yusif was not a favourite with him. He just *did not* like him. To be smart and very popular with everyone was already infuriating. But to see him do so well at archery in such a short space of time was almost too much for him to bear.

It had taken Khalid at least a term of practice at archery club before he could start hitting the target consistently. What with poking his eye as he pulled the arrow back, catching his fingers between the arrow and bow string and missing the target a few hundred times, it had been quite an uphill struggle. Yusif's apparent natural ability at the sport made him feel quite sick!

The three boys from Ibn Majah were watching from the safety of the waiting line, which was five yards behind the shooting line. They had taken a step back for a short break. It was then that an idea popped into Khalid's head. A sly smile swept across his face, overtaking his previous sullen look. He leaned across to the twins after the last arrow in a series of six had been shot, and began to whisper.

The whistle blew.

"*RETRIEVE!*" shouted Ustad Hamza, as it became safe to move across the lawn once more.

The last set of firing was scheduled to be a friendly competition to finish off the day. Sets of arrows had to be shot by each boy, consecutively at the target. At the end of the round, the scores would be added and house points awarded to the winning team. Ustad Hamza proceeded to explain the rules, his voice carrying across the Lower Fields.

"Remember boys, striking the 'X' and inner gold scores you 10 points, outer gold 9, inner red ring 8, outer red 7, inner blue ring 6, outer blue 5, inner black ring 4, outer black 3, inner white ring 2 and outer white 1... A miss scores you no points and is just recorded as 'M'... The top three with the highest total gain points for their respective houses..."

Khalid and the twins walked over towards Yusif and the boys. They had to be quick. As they arrived, Yusif and Daud were alone. Reda and Warsoma had just left them, eager to retrieve their arrows. Warsoma was especially excited, as he had finally succeeded in shooting two of his arrows halfway to the target.

Yusif and Daud were standing squeezing their wrists, which were now beginning to throb with pain. Both boys were suffering from the effects of the friction from the bow as it rubbed against their skin. As beginners to the sport, neither one had managed to avoid this pitfall, that novice archers are all too familiar with. Yusif and Daud both looked up as the others approached.

"You should massage them with warm black seed oil. It works a treat!" said Khalid pointing to their wrists with his bow. "It says so in *Sahih al-Bukhari*. The Prophet said, *'There is healing in the black seed for all diseases except death.'*"

"Really? *Jazakallahu khairan* – I'll do that!" said Yusif.

"I have some on me if you two would like to use it now," said Khalid politely. It was a gesture that took both Yusif and Daud by surprise.

"My mother has an amazing book on the Prophetic medicine. She studied it in Egypt, and she always makes sure I have some black seed oil when I come away to school," said Khalid. He pulled out a small bottle filled with a dark liquid from his trouser pocket. "Of course, it's not warm but it should still help soothe it a bit."

Both Yusif and Daud looked at the bottle. By now their arms were throbbing, and each boy was quite tempted to take up the offer, but Yusif hesitated.

"Oh! We'd like to – but I don't know if we have enough time!" he said. "We should really get the arrows back."

"It's alright..." interrupted Rehan.

"...we can get them for you!" continued Farhan.

Yusif and Daud looked at one another surprised by their offer.

"Thank you, that would be helpful!" replied

Yusif gratefully.

Farhan and Rehan ran across the lawn. Yusif had scored very well again. Five of his arrows had hit the target, and one was on the gold ring. Daud had also done well with three of his arrows on the red ring. As the twins began to pull the arrows off the target, they dropped them casually on to the ground.

They exchanged silent looks with one another and smiled, each apparently aware of the other's thoughts. Then, glancing sneakily over their shoulders back at the others, they made sure no one was watching. They could see Yusif and Daud in the distance, generously applying the black seed oil to their wrists. Both of them were oblivious as to what the twins were up to.

Rehan dropped to his knees as though to pick up the arrows, and Farhan likewise followed suit. Rehan was the first to pick one up. It was Yusif's, bearing the red tail feathers of Ibn Kathir. Holding it between his fingers, he applied firm pressure on the shaft, bending it ever so slightly. Farhan did the same to Daud's arrows.

"There! No one will ever notice unless they look really closely," sniggered Rehan with satisfaction.

Farhan laughed, "Have you finished?"

"Yes, let's get back quickly!" said his mischievous brother.

The twins returned to the shooting line in time to hear the first whistle blow as a signal to clear the field. A brief nod from Rehan told Khalid that they had been successful in their mission. The twins handed over the arrows to Yusif and Daud, then quickly left to take up their own positions on the shooting line.

Khalid took his bottle of black seed oil back from Daud and hastily pushed it back into his pocket before retreating to his original spot. As for Yusif and Daud, they were pleasantly surprised at how effective the black seed oil had been in alleviating their pains. Their arms felt rejuvenated, and they were ready for a final round of shooting.

The whistle blew.

Yusif pulled the string of his bow back and quickly released his arrow. He watched with satisfaction as the arrow travelled swiftly through the air. But this quickly turned to horror as he saw it veer suddenly to the left and, missing the target altogether, embed itself into the grass. He grabbed for his second arrow, aimed and fired. To his astonishment, the result was much the same – another bad miss. This time the arrow implanted itself into the trunk of a nearby Elm tree.

Desperately trying to maintain his composure, Yusif released his final arrow and watched it soar high into the air, as if a gust of wind had taken it up. It eventually found its way into some bushes, narrowly missing a wild rabbit that was grazing in the lower fields.

"*Ya Akhi*, what happened to you? You almost killed a bunny, *astaghfirullah!*" exclaimed Warsoma in disgust, as he turned in shock to look at Yusif. Warsoma of course, was something of a conservationist.

"You're not allowed to kill for sport, *akhi!*"

he warned.

Yusif flushed guiltily.

"I know, I'm sorry!" he said, perplexed. "I don't understand what happened! I swear I aimed straight, but it's like the arrows had a mind of their own!"

"That's ridiculous!" said Warsoma.

"What is?" asked Reda as he joined the two boys, shortly followed by Daud, who himself was looking as frustrated as Yusif.

Yusif began to describe what had happened, but was interrupted by Daud. Having listened to Yusif, Daud had realised that everything Yusif had described had happened to him as well. Although thankfully, he had managed to not come anywhere near innocent living creatures. One of his arrows had even reached Hamudi's target, which was several metres from its intended destination.

Reda silently listened to Yusif's version of the events.

"We need to collect the arrows!" said Reda firmly. There was something so definitive about his tone, that no one dared to dispute his instructions.

"Why, what are you thinking Reda?" asked Yusif curiously.

"No. I need to see the arrows first!" replied Reda abruptly. Without another word, he ran straight out onto the fields, with Yusif hot on his heels. Warsoma and Daud, in the meantime, went together to collect the latter boy's arrows.

By the time Yusif had caught up with Reda, he had found one of the arrows and was busy pulling another out from the bark of the beautiful old Elm tree. Reda examined the arrows with a grim expression across his tight-lipped face. Still he said nothing. He ran on towards the bushes where they were soon joined by Warsoma and Daud, who was clasping his own arrows tightly in his hands.

Reda dropped to his knees in front of the bushes and stuck his hand beneath the undergrowth, searching frantically for Yusif's third arrow. He could see the burrow where the poor little rabbit had sought refuge from Yusif's assault.

Suddenly he let out a cry as his fingers closed around the arrow.

"Got it!" he exclaimed. "Now Daud, give me yours please!" Reda sat on the turf with the six arrows on his lap. Turning each one over, he carefully examined them one by one.

"Well, aren't you going to say anything?" scolded Warsoma raising his arms impatiently into the air.

Yusif and Daud looked at one another. What on earth was Reda doing? What was he looking for?

Finally, Reda stood up and looked at the boys. He held up the arrows in front of them.

"Gentlemen, this is *SABOTAGE*!" he declared, in the most accusing of voices.

Yusif, Daud and Warsoma's mouths fell open in disbelief. Yusif had thought of a variety of possibilities for his wayward aim, such as faulty arrows, a sudden gust of wind, the magnetism of an electric storm...but sabotage! That was just too incredible to contemplate.

"Are you *sure?*" began Yusif in protest. "Maybe you're mistaken, maybe..." But Reda would not hear any of it.

"No! I tell you someone has bent the arrows, so they don't fly straight. See it's bent," insisted Reda, as he held one of Daud's arrows straight out in front of him, straining one eye to look down its shaft. It was the one that had hit Hamudi's target. And sure enough, as all three boys moved in to have a closer look, it certainly did not look straight.

"They're not designed to bend upon impact!" insisted Reda.

"Why would anyone do this?" stammered Daud in shock.

"That's what we need to find out! Now, who handled your arrows other than yourselves?"

Yusif and Daud looked at one another in disbelief and cried in unison, "*THE TWINS* !"

Reda's eyes narrowed as he heard the names. "Are you sure?" he asked. Both boys nodded vigorously.

"Right, let's go!" cried Reda, jumping to his feet.

"Wait, what are you going to do?" asked Warsoma nervously. But Reda was not about to be stopped. He stormed back down the lawn, with the other boys running after him, desperately trying to keep up.

The twins were behind the shooting lines with Khalid, packing away their equipment and loading their arrows into their quivers. They were very pleased with themselves, having done quite well with their scores.

Reda confronted them, his face blazing with anger.

"Did you collect these arrows for Daud and Yusif?" demanded Reda crossly.

The twins looked up with a start. Slowly they stood up, shaking inwardly as they looked nervously at Reda's angry face. When Khalid had encouraged them to bend the arrows, 'just for a joke', they had thought the plan a brilliant one. They had not expected Yusif or Daud to do anything in retaliation. But now, the idea seemed to be much less entertaining. They had forgotten about Reda, with his unstable temperament and constant willingness to stand up for justice! In the face of Reda's furious gesticulations, the courage that had emboldened them to carry out their earlier misadventure deserted them.

"Y-Yes!" stammered Rehan, speaking on behalf of his brother Farhan, who seemed to have been rendered temporarily speechless.

Reda squared his shoulders and pulled himself up to his full 5 feet and 1 inch.

"Did you bend them?" he demanded.

Rehan and Farhan both gulped, with beads of sweat forming on their brows. It was at this point that Khalid stepped forward to their rescue.

"Look, what if they did – what's the harm? It was only a little joke!" suggested Khalid, smiling as sweetly as he could.

"What's the *harm*?" screamed Reda. "I'll tell you what's the harm, it was *stupid*! Somebody could have got hurt. It's sabotage. Vandalism of private property... it's bad sportsmanship, dishonest, it's *haram...!*" he continued, pushing Khalid forcefully back with his heated outburst.

Yusif gasped audibly. He had never seen Reda in such a rage before! Daud stood shell-shocked. Warsoma was moved to say something, but his words failed him. There was nothing anyone could say to Reda when he got into one of his temper tantrums.

Khalid reeled from the force of Reda's push and lost his footing as he fell to the ground with a loud cry.

"Aah! Aah! My ankle! You hurt my ankle!" screamed Khalid noisily, as he rolled on the ground clutching his foot in the most exaggerated manner.

It was at this point that Ustad Hamza came charging up to witness the alarming scene before him. Khalid in pain, was curled up into a ball on the ground, bawling his eyes out. He was surrounded by a mob that looked to be headed by a rather red-faced and fuming Reda.

"*Subhanallah!* What on earth is going on here?" thundered Ustad Hamza.

Chapter Thirteen

Sheikh Ansari

Yusif sat nervously beside Reda, Warsoma and Daud on the old green leather sofa in the school office, just outside Sheikh Ansari's study. Who would have thought that he would find himself in this kind of predicament? He had *never* been in trouble before. To be summoned to the headmaster's office was not at all what he had wanted. What would Ammi think? What of the high hopes his father had held for him? He would be such a disappointment to them. A tear began to well in his eye. It was turning out to be the most intimidating and frightening experience he had ever had. Yusif thought back to the events that took place earlier that day.

* * *

After Ustad Hamza had stormed onto the scene, it had become apparent to everyone that they were in deep trouble. Worse still was the knowledge that Yusif, Reda, Warsoma and Daud were actually the innocent party. However, this fact had somehow been lost in the commotion that played itself out on the field.

Khalid was crying pitifully on the ground,

grasping his ankle. Reda was towering over him, in the most menacing manner. The scene that met Ustad Hamza was a most alarming one. It was not the type of behaviour expected from boys of the Dar Al Ilm Academy. This was clearly a matter for the headmaster's attention.

"It's not fair!" muttered Reda angrily under his breath for the thousandth time. He shuffled uncomfortably in his seat.

"Yes, but if you don't calm down they won't see that!" scolded Warsoma.

"Oh! Put a sock in it!" hissed Reda.

"Shh, will you two!" said Daud, clearly agitated by their squabbling. Just then, the door opened and Sheikh Ansari appeared from the other side.

He looked down at the boys, his face very grave.

"Right, you're here! Well come along boys, in you come!" he instructed in a sombre tone.

The boys stood up gingerly, as Sheikh Ansari held open the door and ushered them into his study.

The room was like an old library, with walls lined with rosewood bookshelves from floor to ceiling. The shelves were filled with volumes and volumes of colourful, leather-bound books. Some looked new, fresh from the printers, whilst others looked like they were from a collection of ancient masterpieces. Various interesting artefacts were dotted about the place, collected from the Sheikh's travels around the Muslim world.

In the centre of the room stood a beautifully carved mahogany desk, laden with paperwork.

Set to one side was a tray of freshly brewed coffee. Its fragrance hung heavily in the air.

As the boys filed into the room, they realised they were not alone. Khalid and the twins were already there. Sheikh Ansari sat down behind his desk on a large, high-backed leather chair. He looked at the boys carefully as they stood, cowering before him. Reda with his fiery expression, Yusif with timid eyes downcast, and Khalid fidgeting anxiously on the spot.

"Well, what happened?" asked Sheikh Ansari, finally ending the unbearably tense silence. Yusif and Daud looked at each other nervously, but Reda was the first to speak up.

"The twins sabotaged Yusif and Daud's arrows, and made them lose the competition!" he blurted. Warsoma rolled his eyes at Reda's rather blunt outburst, fearing it may jeopardise their case.

"Sabotage? How is this so?" asked Sheikh Ansari in amazement.

"They bent the arrows!" replied Reda.

Sheikh Ansari turned to the twins, noting their reluctance to look up.

"Is this true?" he asked sternly. The twins, filled with dread, nodded their heads in admission to the crime.

Sheikh Ansari sat back in his chair in disbelief. Reda smiled for the first time, anticipating that he would soon be vindicated in the matter.

"And whose idea was this?" inquired the Sheikh, his voice ever so slightly raised in tone. Rehan looked hesitantly towards Khalid. But it was the

more submissive sibling of the two who confessed to the truth.

"It was all Khalid's idea!" said Farhan. Khalid flushed as he glanced up at Sheikh Ansari, the guilt written across his face.

"I see. Khalid, was it really you?" asked the Sheikh. Khalid nodded his head.

The Sheikh paused for a moment, and then spoke.

"Boys, what does a Muslim believe is the purpose of life?"

Warsoma raised his hand up in the air. The Sheikh prompted him to answer.

"To seek the pleasure of Allah by worshiping and obeying Him!" replied Warsoma eagerly.

Sheikh Ansari nodded his head, satisfied with the response.

"Correct! And that is exactly what we are trying to achieve here at Dar Al Ilm."

The boys listened quietly.

"Now let me enlighten you about something," he said, glancing across at Khalid and the twins. "You may consider what you have done today to be a small matter. But, in fact, it is a very serious thing," continued the Sheikh, as he began to relate the words of the Prophet, peace be upon him.

"Allah will cause three persons to enter Paradise for one arrow, the maker when he has a good intention in making it, the one who shoots it, and the one who hands it."

The boys listened in earnest. Khalid, Rehan and Farhan hung their heads in shame.

"That's right boys! Bending those arrows was not only a very dangerous act but you may have lost the opportunity for gaining reward. Your actions in damaging those arrows have been contrary to the *sunnah*, and may well have angered Allah." He paused again and looked at them thoughtfully. He reminded the boys that the playing of sports at Dar Al Ilm was not for the sake of seeking the admiration of others.

"We play sports for the good of our health so that we can fulfil our obligations in worshiping Allah, and to prevent ourselves from becoming lazy. It is not something that should lead to petty rivalry or cheating others. We must not forget that in the heat of the competition, as you seem to have done!"

The Sheikh clasped his hands together, one palm in the other, before continuing. "We chose archery in particular to give you the opportunity to seek reward because it has been recommended by our Prophet. I must say that I am very disappointed with you three!"

Khalid and the twins gulped as the Sheikh fixed a look of disapproval upon them.

"You have done wrong, and, for that, your punishment is the opposite of what you had hoped to achieve by your actions. Ten points will be deducted from Ibn Majah House."

Yusif listened quietly. He could not help but feel a little sorry for Khalid and the twins. They looked genuinely upset. Then, Sheikh Ansari turned to the four friends.

"And as for you Reda, there is no excuse for

fighting," he rebuked. Warsoma stole a sideways glance at Reda, whose cheeks flushed.

"Khalid, Rehan and Farhan are your brothers in Islam! You should have reported your concerns about the arrows to Ustad Hamza. There is another saying of the Prophet that you might like to think about. 'When angry, sit down!'"

Reda looked embarrassed. The Sheikh, knowing Reda to have a good heart, sighed. His stern expression softened a little.

"Reda, it's an admirable quality to defend your brother, but it is equally important to maintain your composure and manners at all times, even if you feel that you have been wronged! Your anger has led *you* into trouble."

"I'm sorry Sheikh Ansari," said Reda. The Sheikh nodded his head.

"I'm sure you are son."

The Sheikh asked Khalid and the twins to apologise to Yusif and Daud; as was Reda asked to apologise to Khalid. A strict warning from Sheikh Ansari made it clear to the boys that he never wished to see them again for misbehaviour. Thus admonished, the boys were dismissed.

Outside the headmaster's study, Harun was seated on the green leather sofa. As the boys came out of Sheikh Ansari's room, he jumped with a start to his feet. Although Khalid and the twins noted his presence, they quickly walked off without exchanging a glance.

"What are you doing here?" asked Yusif in surprise

as he looked at Harun's solemn face.

"I didn't hand my maths homework in. It went missing. I lost it...somehow!" replied Harun. "I hope Sheikh Ansari is in a good mood!"

Yusif and the boys gave Harun a sympathetic look and then quickly left the school office. It suddenly dawned on Reda that Harun was in the same house as them.

"Great, that's another point lost for Ibn Kathir!" he mumbled miserably.

Chapter Fourteen

The Vanishing

"That's six people now who seem to have mysteriously lost their homework!" complained Reda as the boys left the prayer hall after *isha* prayers. "Which not only means no house points, but more than likely 'Mr Meany' marks in their place!"

When the boys had awoken that morning, little did they know how bad the day was going to be. It all began after Friday prayers. Shortly after the obligatory two *rakat* of *jumah* had been performed, Sheikh Ansari proceeded to announce the details of the nomination procedure for year captain. It was during the course of his speech that the boys learnt to their dismay, that Ibn Kathir had slipped to fourth place in the results table. That was behind *all* the other houses. Sheikh Ansari had expressed his disappointment about the fact, particularly as they had started the year off in pole position.

"I don't care – it can't be a coincidence, not when six people are involved!" grumbled Reda, as they proceeded across the courtyard. Reda was convinced that foul play was afoot. It did seem strange. After all there was no denying that Ibn Kathir House seemed to be plagued by people losing their homework and assignments. In fact, Harun was not the only one to have found himself waiting outside Sheikh Ansari's room, as he was on the day of the archery incident. After that, it seemed that almost every other day someone from their house was summoned to the headmaster's study.

Furthermore, everyone seemed to have a similar story. One day they would be busy working on an assignment, and the next day it would vanish! You could excuse one, two or even possibly three such occurrences – but six in a month! That was just too much, especially as all the victims were from the same house. As Reda was quick to point out, that was a lot of incidents for one house.

"No, I smell a rat!" exclaimed Reda as he walked with Warsoma and the others back to the dorm room. "Thinking about it now *akhi*, I don't even think your rock pool project got left behind! I think it started with you..."

"What are you saying, Reda?" asked Warsoma incredulously.

"Before your work went missing, we were leading the results table. After your project vanished without a trace, our marks have continued to slip ever since!"

"That's true!" agreed Daud.

"Even your coins, Yusif," continued Reda, "do you really think they fell out of your rucksack?"

Yusif was silent. He had been thinking about it a great deal of late. He had never mentioned it, but he could not understand how they could have gotten lost.

He had recalled the other day when he was in

Ustad Zakariya's class, admiring Khalid's ammonite fossil. It had been placed in a glass display unit next to the teacher's desk, where all the best works were put on show. It was sitting on a velvet cushion that brought out the beautiful patterns on the fossil's surface.

Sighing sorrowfully, Yusif wondered what could have been if he had still had his coins. His mind drifted back to the vivid memory of him carefully wrapping the coins in a white handkerchief, then placing them gently in an inside pocket. He recalled clearly being satisfied at the time that they were safe and secure.

But now after Reda's revelations, he was beginning to wonder if it was possible that he had not lost them after all. Yusif nodded his head in response to Reda's question and proceeded to recount his memories to the boys. Reda was yet more enthused by the positive response of his roommates.

"Imagine what our score points would have been with your coins and Waroma's rock pool project," replied Reda, with satisfaction. "I think someone is deliberately trying to knock us out of the house race!" The boys gasped at the suggestion.

"Why...why would anyone do that?" asked Daud.

"Well – isn't it obvious?" exclaimed Reda as he looked at his friends, all wearing blank expressions. He sighed with exasperation.

"Someone who would want to be year captain very badly!" he said boldly. The boys looked on in shock.

"Hold on – I think that's a bit far-fetched isn't it?" responded Warsoma.

"I agree!" said Yusif. "Surely no one could be *that* desperate?"

"Okay! Then tell me what else it could be?" retorted Reda. The boys looked at one another. But there was no other reason they could think of to explain away the missing work. But why would anyone do such a thing? 'It's so dishonest — it's stealing,' thought Yusif in dismay. 'It's *haram!*'

"Even if they were, who would do such a wrong thing and how were they doing it?" conceded Daud with a puzzled look on his face.

"House members do not have free access to other house dorms."

"Well I can think of someone desperate to be year captain — *Khalid*!" exclaimed Reda. "But how he's doing this I don't know!"

"*Astaghfirullah*, Reda!" exclaimed Warsoma.

"Fear Allah! You cannot cast suspicion upon someone else like that — it's *haram*! You have no proof!" He shook his head in dismay, convinced that everything they had just said was conjecture. We have no real evidence to say foul play has taken place. "For all we know, we shouldn't even be discussing this — it's back biting!" he scolded.

"Fine, if you want proof, we'll follow him then!" cried Reda stubbornly.

"No we will not!" pronounced Yusif flatly. "Are you mad? Don't you know that it's *haram* to spy on your brother?"

Reda looked exasperated. "What then — do we just leave it?" he asked.

"Yes!" replied Yusif calmly. "There is nothing we can do without proof and therefore we have to trust in Allah and pray. Maybe it is not to be in our destiny to win and Allah knows best – right?" replied Yusif, turning towards Warsoma to seek reassurance. Warsoma nodded his head in agreement.

Yusif was perplexed. Everything happened for a reason. His father had always said so. Maybe his earlier concerns were justified – perhaps he was not ready to be year captain and it had therefore been removed from his path. Allah knows best!

Reda shrugged his shoulders. "I guess so," he said glumly. "I'm sorry, you're right."

And so the matter was laid to rest. For the next few days, the boys of Ibn Kathir House ploughed through their work, making every effort to raise points for their house. After all, they still had three weeks to make up lost ground. Mindful of their previous suspicions, they always ensured to lock their work away after they had finished! At least they could try to protect their own individual work if nothing else, and pray to Allah that their efforts would lead to something better.

The boys plodded on, but despite their efforts to forget about the vanishing homework, it was almost a week later that something strange took place to re-open the whole subject again. One evening Yusif, Reda, Daud and Warsoma were returning from the canteen after a supper of pasta in bolognese sauce. It was a particularly mild night, with hardly a single cloud in the sky. Standing outside their dorm entrance, they gazed up at the brilliance of the crescent moon as it shone high above them. On such a clear night as this, there were an unusually large number of stars in the sky. The more the boys looked, the more shimmering stars seemed to appear, until they seemed to almost merge into a white haze.

Suddenly, Daud caught everyone's attention. He had spotted a shooting star as it plunged downwards in the sky with a brilliant tail of light following behind it. Daud loved astronomy. His father was an avid stargazer, and since he had been a young child, Daud had been encouraged to study the heavens above. He never forgot the first time he looked through his father's telescope and saw Saturn with its glorious rings.

Daud stared up at the sky, recalling which planets should be visible at this time in the year, just as his father had taught him. He had seen them so often, that he was able to recognise them in an instant.

"Look up there to the left. See, that's Venus!" said Daud, gesturing enthusiastically up into the sky. He then turned to look in the northeast direction and smiled, "See that star pattern – the one that looks a bit like the letter 'W'. That's the constellation of Cassiopeia!"

"I don't get it, how can you tell the difference between a star and a planet?" asked Warsoma, intrigued by Daud's observation. Daud grinned.

"Oh! That's easy. Choose a star and stare at it hard," he said. "If it twinkles it's a star. If it doesn't then you've found a planet!"

"Wow! That's amazing," gasped Yusif as he took

Daud's advice and picked out a star. "You're right, I found a star!"

"No, what's amazing is you can be lost anywhere in the world and all you have to do is to look at the stars above and you can find your way home!" continued Daud. The boys around him were impressed by Daud's knowledge of the heavenly bodies. They were even more astounded to learn that over 165 stars still have names that are Arabic in origin like Altair, 'The Flying Eagle' and Aldeberan, meaning 'Follower'.

"Muslim astronomers discovered a huge amount about the planetary system, long before the Europeans. In fact, astronomy has always been very important in our religion."

He continued to describe the movements of the sun and moon, and how they are used for timings of prayer and fasting. And how the stars were used for navigation. Daud paused, gazing with eyes as bright as the stars above.

"Did you know that one of the plains on the moon is called 'Messala', after Mashallah ibn Athari, who was a Muslim astronomer way back in the ninth century?"

"*Mashallah!*" exclaimed Warsoma. He was fascinated by this branch of science that was previously unknown to him.

"Yes, that's right, Mashallah ibn Athari," repeated Daud.

"No, I mean *mashallah*, that's amazing!" replied Warsoma.

"Oh, I see, yes...*mashallah!*" laughed Daud.

"You know it was his love for astronomy that drew my father to Islam," he continued.

"What's that?" asked Yusif suddenly, drawing everyone's attention.

Daud looked at Yusif expecting him to have found something of interest in the sky. But to his surprise, Yusif was pointing towards their dorm building, in particular at one of the windows on the ground floor. The curtains in the room were closed but three circular lights could be seen flickering and dancing in the darkness. It was just like watching a firefly dancing in the woods at night.

"That's strange, isn't that Azmi's room?" asked Yusif.

"It is – come on we have to get over there!" cried Reda, as he pushed open the door of the dorm building and ran in.

The boys stormed through the corridor, and arrived outside Azmi's door within moments.

Reda started to knock vigorously on the door.

"Azmi! Azmi! Are you in there?" called Reda. There was no reply. Reda twisted the doorknob. "It's locked!" he exclaimed.

Just then they heard a surprised voice coming from behind them. It was Azmi.

"What's going on *akhi*?"

Chapter Fifteen

Dancing Lights

"Azmi, we saw lights – dancing lights in your room!" explained Warsoma, still panting from the run along the stairs.

"That's impossible, *laa...*" responded Azmi, frowning as he munched on a piece of marmalade toast that he had just made for himself. "No one is in there, and I always switch the lights off when I leave my room!"

"Quickly, open the door – I think there might be someone inside!" ordered Reda anxiously, ignoring Azmi's objections. "Someone *is* inside I tell you, and all this talking is wasting time!"

Azmi moved towards his door as Reda stepped aside to make space for him. Suddenly animated, Azmi pulled out his key, and unlocked the door. Then to the boys' astonishment, he leapt dramatically forward into the room, landing in a martial arts pose, the slice of toast clenched between his teeth. Azmi was an expert in the *silat* style of fighting, and was not afraid to use it.

Reda somewhat impressed by the performance, followed close behind and flicked the light on. The boys scanned the room. It was arranged exactly in the same way as Yusif and the boys' room. There were two bunk beds, study tables and bookshelves on the wall. The only difference being, that the room was in a complete and utter mess!

Azmi, realising that there was no immediate danger, relaxed his posture.

"Oh, my gosh, the place has been ransacked!" exclaimed Daud.

Azmi shuffled uncomfortably on his spot. In fact, the room was always in such a state. He quickly apologised, blaming Harun and Hamudi for their untidiness.

"I don't understand it – we all saw the lights! But there's no one here!" said Reda in frustration.

Yusif crossed the room towards the window that looked out upon the courtyard. He glanced across to the spot where not three minutes ago they had all stood gazing up at the stars above. He examined the window – it was locked and looked undisturbed. There was no sign to suggest that an intruder had used the window to get in or out. Turning around to look back at the room, he smiled as he saw Reda on the floor checking under the bed.

"Did you find anything?" laughed Yusif.

Reda shook his head as he emerged from under the bunk.

"Just some old socks, chocolate wrappers and a mouldy scone!" reported Reda, most disappointed.

Suddenly Azmi cried out in dismay. All eyes turned to look at him. He was stood by his desk, clutching a piece of paper in his hands.

"Where's the rest of my essay? It's gone!" cried Azmi, with a look of utmost anguish on his face. He had spent a good part of the day writing a short story for Ustad O'Malley's English homework. It was the best piece of work he had done so far, and Azmi had been much relieved when he had finally completed it.

"Are you sure?" asked Warsoma. "Could you have put it away somewhere and forgotten about it?"

"No – it's impossible!" he replied. "I just finished it half an hour ago. I was so busy working on it all day that I didn't even have a chance to eat. As soon as I wrote the last sentence, I got up and left to get a snack from the kitchen. I left the papers right here on the desk. And you all saw that the door was locked!"

Azmi was right. The boys had indeed found the door locked and the window closed too. It just did not make any sense. Everyone present started to frantically search the room, in the vain hope of finding the missing papers. As their search drew to an end, the possibility of solving the mystery looked less and less likely. It was then that Daud made an unexpected discovery.

"Look, I've found something!" he cried as he crouched low on the floor near the wardrobe. The others gathered curiously around him. Looking over Daud's shoulder, they could see a dirty mark smudged on the wooden floorboard.

"What does that look like to you?" asked Daud, excitedly.

"Why, it's a footprint!" exclaimed Azmi in surprise.

"None of our shoes are this dirty," said Yusif. "Do you think it's yours, or maybe Harun's or Hamudi's?"

Azmi looked surprised. He studied the dirty black footprint carefully. There was a peculiar zigzag pattern made by the sole of the shoe.

"No, it's not mine, and I don't think it's theirs. The footprint is too big!" confirmed Azmi. "Besides, Harun and Hamudi might keep the room untidy, but none of us ever wear our shoes inside!" insisted Azmi. He proudly pointed to the shoe rack that stood next to their dorm door. Sure enough, the rack was full of the shoes that the room occupants owned. On closer inspection, Warsoma confirmed that none of them had dirty black soles or zigzag patterns.

"I knew it!" shouted Reda triumphantly. "This is the proof we need. An intruder must have been here!"

"No, not really..." advised Warsoma sceptically.

"Someone might have visited and left it a while ago. So it doesn't really prove anything!" he suggested, somewhat dampening Reda's enthusiasm.

But it was true. The teachers would probably say that. Nonetheless, Reda was adamant. He had to admit that a simple footprint did not mean someone was out to ruin Ibn Kathir House by stealing homework! The only way to prove it would be to catch the intruder red-handed.

"What are you all talking about?" asked Azmi, intrigued by the boys' discussion. Yusif glared at Reda, as he moved to open his mouth and was just about to spill the beans about his suspicions.

"Oh, it's nothing Azmi, just silly talk!" said Yusif quickly, before Reda had a chance to speak. "I'm sorry about your work. It's not a big problem, at least you still have another day to redo the pages!"

Azmi sighed, "I suppose so, *laa*. I guess it was Allah's will."

With this, the boys quickly left for their own dorms. Azmi was left behind, a little bewildered by the proceedings of the evening. But, before long, he turned his attention to Ustad O'Malley's English homework – again.

* * *

The last days of term passed by, and it was finally the day of the house nominations. The boys of year seven sat quietly cross-legged in the prayer hall. There were four wooden ballot boxes at the end of the hall, one for each house. Everyone had been given a white sheet of paper to write the names of three boys they thought would be the best to represent their house as year captain.

Yusif sat looking expectantly around at the boys in his house. They were not allowed to discuss the nominations with each other. It was just as well for Yusif, as he was still uncertain about whether he should stand or not, and discussing the matter again would have created even more confusion in his mind. The last thing he wanted was to have people coming up to him and asking him a million questions. Despite this, Yusif still felt like a goldfish in a bowl.

He was very much conscious of eyes looking at him from time to time.

Yusif looked at his paper. He had pencilled in Warsoma and Azmi. Reda, as much as he liked him, was just not quite right for the role. No doubt, he had many good qualities such as being loyal, dependable and strong. But he was just too hot-headed at times. He had a tendency to act on impulse and think later. Not ideal traits for a leader, Yusif felt.

As for Daud, he definitely had the brains and the potential, but right now he needed to grow in confidence. Nobody else seemed to stand out for the job. Not Harun, Hamudi and certainly not Zulfi!

No, both Warsoma and Azmi were the most sensible choices. They were God-fearing, always wanting to help others and mindful of doing good. They were both intelligent, level headed, trustworthy, and kind hearted. In fact, for Yusif they were the most sincere people he had ever known! They never pretended to be anything more or anything less than what they were.

Yusif chewed the back of his pen. Then there was himself. Should he put his *own* name forward? A part of him wanted to, and rise to the challenge. Another part shied away through fear. He closed his eyes, and made *dua*, seeking direction from Allah about what he should do.

He had already performed the *istikharah* prayer asking for guidance from Allah, just as Abdul Kadir had advised him one day, when he chanced by him in the library. Abdul Kadir had told him that it was a special prayer, where one performs two *rakat* and then reads a short *dua* seeking guidance in a matter that one is unsure about.

"It's simple – you might get a dream or even just a feeling! But the important thing is that whatever decision you make, whatever the outcome, you left it to the judgement of Allah to decide what was best for you."

Yusif slowly began to write his own name. But as he got to the third letter 's' he stopped, overwhelmed by a sense of unease. Suddenly, a strong feeling struck him. At that moment, he resolved that he would not nominate himself. He had done *istikharah*. If he were destined for the job, then the other boys' nominations would be enough. More importantly, it would reflect their confidence in him. And that would be the best way. After all it is a big responsibility to represent one's classmates. If *they* trusted him, then he would accept it. But if it was not good for him to be year captain, then Allah would remove it from his path!

With this thought, he scribbled his name out, then stood up and marched straight up to the wooden ballot box for Ibn Kathir House. The house emblem was painted onto the front, and there was a slot for the papers to be dropped through at the top. There was no turning back. The matter was now in Allah's hands. He lifted his chin up with confidence, said 'bismillah', and dropped the paper through the slot.

"There, it's done!" said Yusif to himself.

A whole hour had passed by before the boys were eventually allowed to leave the prayer hall.

Afternoon classes had been suspended to allow all the year groups in the school to take part in the nominations for their respective years. It was a particularly warm afternoon, and the boys were in desperate need to cool down and wash away the stresses of the day. Swimming seemed to be the ideal activity, so Yusif and the boys decided to go down to the school swimming pool, after their voting was done.

Yusif and Reda raced up and down the pool, leaving the others content to practise diving – or 'belly flops' in the case of Warsoma. Azmi and Hamudi showed up a little later, and challenged them all to see who could stay under the water holding their breath for the longest period. The boys couldn't resist. They all formed a circle in the pool.

"After three," said Hamudi. "One, two, three... go!"

All six heads ducked under the water. Yusif's eyes blurred over for a second then began to focus, adjusting to the water. They were waving at one another under the pool, except Hamudi who was eagerly pulling faces in an effort to make the others laugh and lose the contest.

Poor Warsoma was the first to resurface. Then Azmi, shortly followed by Daud and Yusif. Despite his best efforts to distract the others, Hamudi resurfaced, making Reda the winner. Reda sprung up from the water cheering and revelling in his victory.

Yusif floated himself in the water, smiling as he watched the spectacle before him. Whatever the outcome of the nominations, he had truly come to enjoy the school and his new friends, and looked forward to carrying on there with or without the title of year captain. A sudden jolt brought him back to the present. He gasped for a moment as he felt himself pushed. A float carrying someone collided firmly into him, causing him to briefly submerge into the water. It was Khalid.

"Hey, watch where you're going!" cried Yusif spluttering, as his hands moved automatically to push the float away.

"Oh, I'm so sorry *akhi*, I didn't plan to come your way!" protested Khalid innocently.

"Are you alright?" asked Reda as he came to Yusif's side having witnessed the collision.

"Yes, I'm not hurt," assured Yusif.

"You should be more careful, Khalid!" scolded Reda. But Yusif stopped him from speaking any further. After all it was just an accident, and Khalid had apologised. Reda sniffed his nose reluctantly. Khalid smiled. He was about to move away but seemed to change his mind. He turned towards Yusif again.

"So how do you think you'll do in the nominations?" asked Khalid, unable to resist.

"What do you mean?" replied Yusif.

"I think you might be a popular choice for your house!" said Khalid.

"How would you know?" interjected Reda.

"Oh! It's just that I've overheard his name dropped quite a few times over the last couple of weeks. I just wondered if you knew?"

"Well I didn't, and it doesn't really matter," said Yusif.

"I guess you're right," continued Khalid. "It doesn't matter, because I don't think Ibn Kathir House is going to win. You've all done well to move up to second place. But I can't see you making it back to top of the table in one week!"

It was true. It was very unlikely that their house could make up the lost points. But there was something very unkind about the way that Khalid spoke. As he glided away on his float, paddling with his hands, Yusif could not help but wonder about Khalid. Why did he have to be so unpleasant?

For the first time he could not help but wonder at Reda's suspicions. After all Khalid was involved in the sabotage of the arrows, so that his house would win the archery competition. Could it be possible that he was capable of doing something even more sinister to win the house competition? Yusif shook his head at the crazy notion. 'No, that is just silly!' he thought to himself. I must have been deprived of air for too long under the water. He and his classmates from Ibn Kathir House would just have to buckle down and work hard for the next week – and pray. After all, anything is possible for Allah.

For the most part, the next week passed by uneventfully. The boys made their last efforts. Extra care was given to their assignments; more time was spent in the library and less in the common room. Everything seemed to be going smoothly for Ibn Kathir House – that is, until late Friday evening!

Yusif and the boys were on the way back from the library. They had spent the whole afternoon and a good part of the evening working on an assignment for Ustad Zakariya, who had issued a particularly challenging task about the ecosystem.

Feeling especially tired and starving from all their brainwork, they were on their way back to the dorms to drop off their books, before heading towards the canteen. As they strolled through the courtyard, Daud suddenly froze on the spot, his mouth agape as he stared at their dorms ahead.

"Are you okay *akhi*, what's wrong?" asked Reda, noticing the sudden pallor of Daud's complexion.

Daud pointed his finger unsteadily towards their dorms and whispered.

"Look, that's our room isn't it?"

Reda, Yusif and Warsoma all turned to look towards their window. Their eyes widened as they saw the same 'dancing lights' they had seen a week ago through Azmi's window. Only this time it was in *their* room!

"*Subhanallah!*" exclaimed Warsoma.

"Come on, we have to be quick. This may be our only chance!" shouted Reda over his shoulder as he sprinted across the courtyard. The others followed, hearts thumping wildly as they made a rush for their room. There was no mistaking what Reda had implied. This might be the only chance they had to solve the mystery behind the lights. Now they would see for themselves if there really was an intruder!

The boys reached the door to their room in almost

no time. There were sounds coming from inside. Reda quickly unlocked the door.

"Ready!" he whispered, turning to look at the boys standing behind him. The others nodded. They were too terrified to speak, unsure as to what they might find.

Reda pushed the door open and switched on the light. There was a loud gasp, as the boys watched the mystery 'dancing light' fade into the darkness of the wardrobe. The door slammed shut.

Chapter Sixteen

Caught!

"*Subhanallah!* What was that?" cried Warsoma. Reda ignored him. He charged across the room towards the fitted oak wardrobe and pulled the doors wide open. The clothes were hanging curiously squashed to one side of the rail.

"What's going on?" exclaimed Yusif, standing behind Reda, who, himself, had climbed into the wardrobe. Other than the clothes, it was empty. Reda was busy running his hands up and down the back of the wardrobe wall. Yusif was also searching around, and noticed an object on the floor. He knelt to the floor and scooped it up – it was a torch!

"Reda, look, this doesn't belong to us!" he cried. "Here's the source of your dancing lights. It's a torch!"

Briefly distracted, Reda examined the object with a puzzled expression. "There has to be a secret opening here...or something!" he insisted.

In his frustration, he thrust his clenched fist against the back of the wardrobe. Suddenly, the back panelled wall seem to give way under the impact. A sudden gust of cold air wisped across their faces, making a howling sound as it passed them. A large, dark space appeared to open up in front of their eyes. Reda and

Yusif stared at each other, astonished.

"What is this place?" exclaimed Warsoma. It was a question that was on everyone's mind, as they stared into the darkness.

"*Ya Allah*, it's a secret passage!" cried Daud, who was by this time, craning his neck to look over Yusif's shoulder.

"Warsoma, and Daud! Go and fetch Ustad Ibrahim," ordered Reda, taking the lead. "Yusif, you come with me!"

Without a further thought, Reda stooped his head and stepped into the passage. Yusif followed hot on his heels, leaving Warsoma and Daud staring after them in a daze. It was pitch black inside. Yusif instinctively lifted the torch and fumbled to find the switch. He flicked it on, and the tunnel illuminated before them. The two boys looked on in amazement. The tunnel looked centuries old! The walls were made up of large stones, cut into blocks. The ground was uneven, dirty and black, obviously the source of the footprint left behind in Azmi's room. A few feet in front, was a spiral staircase, leading down to a lower level.

"Let's go!" whispered Reda.

Yusif hesitated for a moment, wondering if they should wait for the teacher. But curiosity got the better of him, and he nodded to Reda. As he started to take a step forward, Reda felt his foot knock against something. He stumbled to the ground.

"Yusif!" cried Reda as he fell down to his knees.

* * *

"*Akhi*, are you alright?" asked Yusif as he crouched down beside Reda. Yusif shone the torch down towards the floor, offering a hand to help his fallen companion. It was then that the boys' eyes fell upon the object Reda had stumbled upon. It was a brown cardboard box, overturned by Reda, with some of its contents spilt out onto the floor of the tunnel.

There before them, lay the old coins, shimmering in the torchlight, still half-wrapped in a handkerchief.

"My coins!" gasped Yusif.

"I knew it! I knew I couldn't have lost them at the beach!"

Looking closer, the boys found numerous other objects that had been placed into the box. There was an Arabic grammar book, scissors, a dictionary, and various homework sheets – all apparently belonging to boys from Ibn Kathir House!

Their attention shifted from the box to the sudden sound of footsteps, fading off into the far distance.

"Come on, we have to hurry!" cried Reda as he grabbed Yusif by his arm and pulled himself up to his feet.

They cautiously made their descent down the stairwell, ears ringing with the sound of their feet clanging on the rusty old iron steps. After a few moments, they had reached what appeared to be the mouth of a large tunnel. They stood transfixed, as they looked at the vast expanse that opened up before them. Reda boldly charged forward.

A damp, mouldy smell hung in the air, which reminded Yusif of the old cellar in the basement of his grandfather's house. As he ran, he felt his face brush past cobwebs that hung low from the roof of the tunnel. Yusif's skin crawled. He had never been in such a place before, and part of him felt quite afraid. He could still hear the sounds of his footsteps echoing all around him. It was an eerie, hollow sound that made the hair on the back of his neck stand on end. Suddenly they stopped dead in their tracks.

The tunnel in front of them split into two branches. By this time, they must have run at least fifty feet away from their room. Who would have thought such a place could exist beyond the confines of their wardrobe? The boys stood staring into the darkness of the tunnels before them, which were only just visible from the light of the torch. They listened hard for the sound of the footsteps, or any small indication as to which way they should go. But all they could hear was the sound of slow dripping water, and the occasional gust of wind.

"What do we do? Which way do we go?" asked Reda looking helplessly from one tunnel to the other. "Perhaps we should split up."

Yusif pointed the torch from one tunnel to the other. Something was amiss, but he could not quite figure out what it was. For the next few seconds, he stood carefully studying the tunnels.

Then in a flash, he knew what it was. He remembered a story that his father had read to him at bedtime when he was younger. It was about the time when the Prophet Muhammad and his close companion Abu Bakr were travelling to Medina, at the time of the *hijrah* from Makkah. They were leaving the persecution they had suffered in their homeland, and were being chased by enemies who were determined to kill them. They sought refuge in a small cave called *al-thawr*, and were about to be discovered.

Yusif recalled how he would sit mesmerised in his bed, his blanket held close around him, wondering what would happen next. Would the enemies of the Prophet follow them into the cave? Would they escape unharmed?

"But Abu, wouldn't Allah help him?" he asked his father.

"That's exactly what Abu Bakr had wondered, and so he began to pray," answered Abu. "The Prophet heard him, and reassured him that Allah would help them."

"And did he?" asked Yusif anxiously.

"Yes, he did – he sent a spider to his rescue," smiled Abu.

"A spider? How can a spider defeat men?" Yusif asked, most surprised by his father's explanation. Abu looked at him and smiled.

"*Subhanallah* Yusif! What more proof would you need to recognise Allah's greatness? For only He could summon a creature such as a spider to defeat the greatest of foes, despite their weapons and strength. Anything is possible for Allah. He has only to say 'be!' and it is. Allah is not bound by the natural laws as we are. He is the one that created them in the first place.

It is a matter of faith. Do you understand Yusif?" Yusif nodded.

It was a story that Yusif had never forgotten. His father had described how the spider had helped the Prophet by building a web at the mouth of the cave. This fooled the enemies of the Prophet into thinking that the web had been there for a long time. They left without looking into the cave, assuming that it would have been impossible for anyone to enter without disturbing the spider's web.

Yusif turned his attention back to the tunnel in which he was standing. He now realised what was amiss.

"It's the left one!" he exclaimed. "The cobwebs are broken, and there are very little of them left. So whoever, or *whatever* we are chasing, must have passed through the left one! See, the other tunnel looks like it has never been used." A smile appeared on Reda's excited face, as he realised precisely the same thing.

"Yes, you're right! Well spotted, *akhi*," he said.

The boys entered the tunnel to the left, and continued their chase. The footsteps they were following returned once more, gradually becoming louder and louder. They were making headway and before long, they could see the shadow of a person. It was flickering menacingly now on the walls as he ran to make his escape.

"STOP!" cried Yusif breathlessly. But it was useless, as the culprit was determined to get away. Reda and Yusif somehow found the energy to step up their pace.

It was on hearing their thundering footsteps, that the intruder made a fatal error of judgement. He turned to look over his shoulder to see how far away his pursuers were. Losing his footing, he tripped and fell to the ground with a loud cry.

He tried to drag himself up off the ground, but it was too late − he was *caught*! Reda pounced upon him, pushing him back down to the ground. Within moments, Yusif had arrived by Reda's side. Reda was desperately trying to pin the intruder to the ground as he struggled to break free.

"Here, help me Yusif!" gasped Reda.

Reda pulled the intruder's arms behind his back. Yusif knelt down trying to catch his breath for a second, before he too placed his own hands on the intruder's shoulders, holding him down. Unable to fight against the two of them, the intruder finally gave up the struggle and lay limp, face down on the ground.

Just then, the boys heard footsteps running towards them. Two figures appeared from in front of them, with torches blazing light into their eyes. Yusif and Reda looked away for a second in pain. Their eyes had become accustomed to the darkness, and they were for a moment unable to tolerate the glare. Reda protested noisily. Yusif quickly picked up his own torch and pointed it back at the newcomers. He gasped as he recognised their faces. It was *Rehan* and *Farhan*!

It was then that Yusif looked down at the motionless figure lying on the ground before him, with a growing anticipation as to who it might be. He gently turned the intruder to face them. In an instant, he recognised who it was that they had been following. It was Khalid!

"Khalid, you sneak!" cried Reda.

Khalid stared back, eyes wide open in shock and fear. His face was dirty and tear-stained, his expression one of terror and guilt all rolled into one.

"*Subhanallah!* What on earth is happening here?" blasted a familiar voice. Reda and Yusif turned to look back over their shoulders in the direction from where they had come. It was Ustad O'Malley, with Ustad Ibrahim close behind.

Chapter Seventeen

Confession

Yusif stood nervously beside Reda in the headmaster's study once again. Khalid, Rehan and Farhan were also there, looking downcast. None of them had ever seen Sheikh Ansari annoyed. This was far worse than the time before, when they had stood in the same place just a few weeks ago over the archery incident.

However, Sheikh Ansari was not shouting, as the boys had feared he would. In fact, it was his quietness that made it all the more terrifying. Instead, he was seated before them looking very thoughtful. There was the faintest tinge of red in his ordinarily pale cheeks, which was perhaps the only sign that indicated a change in his mood. He listened silently to Ustad O'Malley's account.

The narration began from the moment Warsoma and Daud were stood panting for breath outside Ustad Ibrahim's office, where they found him and Ustad O'Malley talking together. He heard how the boys were claiming to have discovered tunnels in the dorm rooms, and that Reda and Yusif had gone along them in pursuit of an intruder. Ustad O'Malley described the events up to the point where the five boys were discovered at the end of the tunnel.

After the full account had been given, the room was filled with a most uncomfortable silence. The teachers looked at the boys, and each boy stood wishing that the earth would swallow him up. Yusif gulped. For the first time, he considered that entering the tunnel in such haste might not have been the wisest thing to do. His thoughts then turned to his parents – what would they make of all this? Why did he have to act on an impulse? It was so unlike him. But then again he was not in the most normal of circumstances. After all, it is not every day that you discover secret tunnels in the back of your wardrobe! He only prayed that Sheikh Ansari would also see it that way.

Sheikh Ansari looked at the old cardboard box sitting on the large oak desk before him. It was the same box that Yusif had stumbled over in the tunnel. He sifted through its contents until he discovered the coins. Picking them out, he began to examine them carefully, with great interest. Slowly he looked up, his head shaking, and broke the silence as he addressed the boys.

"Never, in all my thirty years of teaching have I had to deal with anything like this," he said. "How did you come by these tunnels, and what were you all doing there?" he continued, quite calmly. The boys could tell from his tone that all was not well.

Reda had been anxiously awaiting this moment. Now that it had come, there was no holding him back. He launched into his accusations.

"Khalid and the twins have been using the tunnels to steal our class assignments!" he blurted. "All of the missing things belong to the boys of Ibn Kathir, and he wanted us to lose house points. The items in that box came from our rooms!" He pointed to the box, and continued his explanation.

"You see, those coins are the ones Yusif found on Hastings beach. Yusif had thought they had been lost!" he continued, glaring at Khalid and the twins with disdain.

Sheikh Ansari looked at Yusif, holding the coins in his outstretched hand. "Do these belong to you Yusif?" he asked.

Yusif nodded his head, looking towards Ustad O'Malley, as if to seek corroboration. Ustad O'Malley confirmed that they were the ones that Yusif had shown to him on the beach on the day of the field trip. Sheikh Ansari then turned his attention to Khalid, who stood petrified before him. The twins began to squirm a little on their spot.

"Well Khalid, there have been some very serious allegations made against you and your friends," said the Sheikh sternly. "Did you boys remove these items from their room?"

"Yes, Sir..." sniffed Khalid, admitting to the truth. Since being discovered in the tunnels, Khalid had been thinking long and hard about his behaviour. He had realised that there was no escaping the truth of what he had done. He had been found out and it was time to own up and take the blame.

"It was my idea, not the twins," he added, his head bowed down towards the floor in guilt. The twins looked at each other and sighed with relief. Sheikh

Ansari shook his head.

"*Subhanallah!* Why would you do such a wicked thing?" asked the Sheikh incredulously. Khalid could not meet the Sheikh's eyes.

"I – I wanted Ibn Majah to win, so I could have the chance to be year captain," stammered Khalid, feeling terrible about his actions. The idea had not seemed so bad at the time, but looking back now as he stood in front of the headmaster, he realised it *was* a wicked and deceitful scheme. What could possibly have possessed him to do such a thing?

"But, Khalid," said the Sheikh, "stealing is *haram*, and you sought to win through dishonest means. Your actions are nothing but an indication that you are *not* worthy of the responsibility! A captain must have *taqwa*, fear of Allah, and integrity." Khalid looked on in distress.

"But I – I didn't think it was stealing!" pleaded Khalid sincerely. "I didn't keep those things for myself. I left everything in the box just on the other side of the secret door. I was going to return them, really I was..."

"No, Khalid – " corrected Sheikh Ansari. "Just because you did not take the things for yourself, it does not stop it from being stealing. Those things were not your property to remove in the first place – therefore it *was* stealing!"

At this point, Khalid realised that there really could be no excusing his actions. He hung his head, shame-faced. He had honestly not considered his actions to be stealing, but now he felt miserable and full of remorse. He sniffed his nose loudly, trying his best not to cry. Yusif looked at him with sympathy. Khalid was a little self-absorbed, but he did not believe him to be a bad person. After all, he seemed genuinely sad, and that must mean something.

The Sheikh asked how Khalid and the twins had come to know about the tunnels. It was something that everyone in the room was interested to know. And so Khalid began his story.

He described his conversation with Saqib Khan the day they had met at the fountain after *tajweed* class. Khalid had been intrigued by the rumours about old passageways in the grounds of the Academy. He had felt certain that they existed, thinking there could be no smoke without fire.

Saqib had told him that several years ago, a boy from Ibn Majah had supposedly claimed to have found tunnels in the basement of their dorms. The dorms of Ibn Majah were in one of the oldest parts of the school buildings. Khalid explained how on his first day he had stumbled upon a door at the end of one of the corridors, which he had mistaken for the kitchen. But Ustad Zakariya had quickly stopped him, saying the door led to the basement. It had been used as a cellar in the old days, but now it was just used as a storeroom. It was out of bounds for pupils.

Khalid had decided to go down to the basement the very same evening he had spoken with Saqib. It took some time, but with Rehan and Farhan's help, they had managed to find a hidden door at the back of an old cupboard. It was cleverly concealed behind the panels. They would have missed it if it had not been for a peculiar sound coming from the other side of the panels. It was the sound of wind, which whistled ever so softly.

Khalid had knocked on the back panels and sure enough, they sounded hollow. After a thorough examination of the panels, he eventually found the mechanism to open them. It was a simple latch controlling a secret door. The rest was history.

In the weeks that had followed, Khalid and his chums had explored the tunnels whenever they could. Sometimes they left dinner early, or woke up very early in the morning before the others. Their absences had gone unnoticed. They found that through the tunnels, they were able to access many rooms around the school, such as the dorms of the different houses and even Sheikh Ansari's room, which they had once entered through a secret door behind the bookcase. Sheikh Ansari himself, who looked visibly alarmed at the prospect that his room could be accessed so easily, did not welcome this piece of news.

It was beginning to dawn on Khalid that he was in for some serious trouble. Trembling, he turned to look at Sheikh Ansari. He mustered all the strength he could in his heart, and spoke in earnest.

"I'm really very sorry, sir. You see, Ibn Kathir House were in the lead, and I...I wanted our house to win. I wanted a chance to be the year captain so..." he hesitated, as if on the brink of making some great confession. "I wanted to be the year captain so the other boys would *like* me!"

He had finally said it. His eyes searched desperately

for signs of understanding or clemency in the Sheikh's eyes. He felt a sinking feeling deep in the pit of his stomach, and an uncomfortable realisation of the gravity of his actions dawned upon him.

To him, his reasons had never sounded so weak and terrible as they did right now, as he stood before everyone. Khalid bit his lip in an effort to hold back his tears, as his eyes began to water. But a solitary tear managed to escape and trickle its way down his cheek. Khalid brushed it away quickly, a gesture that did not go unnoticed.

Sheikh Ansari sighed to himself, and softened his tone a little.

"Khalid, is that what you really think being year captain is all about? Popularity?" he asked. "For if you do, then young man, you are very much mistaken."

Khalid stood quietly, unable to reply. Yusif and Reda exchanged helpless looks. By now both boys had heard enough of the incredible story to realise that Khalid had just simply made a terrible mistake. For Reda and Yusif it was a revelation. They realised that behind all his apparent confidence, Khalid felt just as insecure as anyone of the rest of them. It seemed hard to be angry with anyone who acted for the sake of being liked by others.

Both boys had to admit that throughout their time at the Academy they had made no real effort to get to know Khalid. This was not the spirit of brotherhood expected of a Muslim.

"Khalid, please think about this," said Sheikh Ansari.

He explained how the Messenger of Allah once cautioned a Muslim who sought a position of leadership. The Prophet advised him not to seek it as he felt that the man was unsuitable for such a role. The man was warned that if he sought it, he would receive no help from Allah.

"So you see just because you may want to be a leader, it does not necessarily make you the best person to be one!"

The Sheikh paused for a moment and looked at Khalid kindly.

"We encourage students to come forward for important positions, but only with the right intentions and always with a strong sense of responsibility and duty."

The Sheikh stood up and walked to Khalid's side. He gently placed his hand on his shoulder and offered him a clean handkerchief. Khalid took the crisp white cloth and rubbed his eyes vigorously.

"Khalid, it is not rank or position that makes people like or respect you. It is your *iman,* honesty, sense of duty and good manners towards others. Only then will you gain their trust – or even friendship."

Khalid listened carefully to the Sheikh's words.

"The blessed Prophet was given the name *al-Amin,* the trustworthy, by his community out of love and respect for him, long before he ever became a leader. Allah gave him a noble character and entrusted the message of Islam to him. Many people embraced Islam because of this and welcomed the Prophet as their leader, like the people of the *Ansar.*"

Khalid and the boys knew this, of course. Had they not been taught on many occasions that the Prophet was the best of all creation and the best example to follow?

"Judging by your behaviour and what we have heard today, I can only conclude that your intentions were so clouded, that you could no longer see what was right from wrong," continued the headmaster.

Khalid nodded his head, realising what a grave mistake he had made. Like Yusif, the Sheikh did not believe that Khalid was bad. The competition between the houses was supposed to encourage students to work hard and do their best. He had never dreamt it would lead to cheating.

"You are still young Khalid," said Sheikh Ansari, now in a much more encouraging voice. "I do not think you realised what you were doing. Stealing and cheating are forbidden in Islam. And it is important that you live your life as Allah has ordered."

In fact, the Sheikh had been thinking hard about how to deal with the situation. By this time, his mind was made up. There was only one thing he could do.

"All the homework removed will have to be submitted and marked," he announced. "I will discount the points raised by Khalid and the twins, and make up the points for the boys who had 'lost' their homework."

Reda was elated by the Sheikh's decision. He was not sure how these changes would affect the scores of the different houses, but he felt certain that it would put Ibn Kathir House in with a chance of winning.

With this ended Yusif's most daunting day at Dar Al Ilm Academy. Sheikh Ansari had decided to formally investigate the tunnels and decide whether they should be sealed up, or if some productive use could be made of them. In the meantime, he had given clear instructions to all present never to talk about or reveal the whereabouts of the tunnels to anyone in the school. Naturally, the boys agreed to all the conditions imposed upon them, happy to hear that they were not to be severely punished for their actions.

After the boys had gone, the remaining teachers discussed the issue at some length.

"But there were no evidence of tunnels in the old plans," insisted Ustad O'Malley, perturbed by the knowledge of their existence. "It doesn't make any sense!"

Ustad O'Malley realised that the tunnels would have to be dealt with first. It would mean that a good part of the summer holidays would have to be used making the necessary arrangements. What a set back to the renovation work!

Sheikh Ansari then smiled sympathetically at Ustad O'Malley, his eyes twinkling with amusement.

"Why, I don't know about that – it makes perfect sense to me," he chuckled. "After all, they wouldn't *be* 'secret' tunnels if they had been drawn in the plans!"

Chapter Eighteen

And the
Year Captain is...

As always, Sheikh Ansari was true to his word.
Three days after the tunnel incident, the homework
and assignments were marked, and the house scores
were appropriately revised. Points had been deducted
from Ibn Majah House, and added to Ibn Kathir.
The rest of the school were not informed of the full
reasons for the changes, other than that some of the
boys from the house had earned misdemeanour marks
for a serious offence and that missing homework had
been recovered and marked.

Every effort was made to conceal the antics of
Khalid and the twins. Sheikh Ansari felt it only
prudent to do so. After all, it was not wise for everyone
to know about the tunnels and, more importantly,
hearing about the incident may influence further
inappropriate behaviour. It was also to protect
Khalid and the twins from criticism from their peers.
They had apologised, repented and learned their
lesson – of that Sheikh Ansari felt sure! It is
never a good thing to reveal the faults or bad
actions of other Muslims.

Before long, the day of the formal announcement of the house results had arrived. It was also the day that the boys would know from which house the year captain was to be chosen. There was a buzz of excitement in the school, as all the teachers and pupils of the Dar Al Ilm Academy assembled in the main hall. Sheikh Ansari opened the proceedings with some wise words.

"As Muslims, we should be leaders, and in the words of our beloved Prophet, may peace be upon him, 'All of you are shepherds, and each of you will be asked concerning his flock.'"

"We need strong leaders from amongst us who will stand up for the cause of Allah, and care for the wellbeing of others. At Dar Al Ilm, we desire for you all to strive to be the best that you can be. We wish for you to exemplify all manner of good Islamic qualities and principles and to follow in the great steps of the noble Messenger of Allah, whom we know was the best of all creation. He was the best servant of Allah, the best of teachers sent to mankind, the best leader, the best to his family and the very best in every aspect of life. We should, therefore, want to do good deeds and help others."

"To be year captain is a huge responsibility. Whosoever is chosen must care for the wellbeing and needs of his fellow students. So boys, I advise you to choose your year captain wisely. As for the captain himself, you should step forward with courage and humility, and be aware of your duty to Allah.

Much to Reda's delight, and that of his roommates,

Ibn Kathir House rose through the ranks and came in at first place. To Yusif's amazement, he himself had received a large number of nominations to stand for year captain. Perhaps this was the answer to his *istikharah* prayer? He could not think of any real reason for not standing now.

Sheikh Ansari's words had struck a chord within Yusif. He continued to be in two minds about the position of year captain, now that the prospect was becoming more and more realistic. The next day Sheikh Ansari summoned him to his office. The inside of the great study was by now an all too familiar site to Yusif, but this time his reasons for being there were more legitimate – although no less daunting! Before him was a panel that consisted of the four housemasters, Abdul Kadir as the head boy and, of course, Sheikh Ansari himself. The purpose of the meeting was to invite Yusif to accept his nomination as year eight captain. This would put him in the running against other colleagues from Ibn Kathir House. The masters themselves had approved the choice, and all that remained was for Yusif to accept the proposal.

"Well Yusif, you have indeed achieved a great deal in your first year at Dar Al Ilm," said Sheikh Ansari warmly.

"Not only have you settled in and performed well in your studies, but you have managed to gain a very good standing amongst your colleagues."

"Yes, Sir," replied Yusif, a little embarrassed. "And I am grateful to everyone here for having welcomed me."

"All that remains now is to ask if you feel you would be willing to take up the position that you have been nominated for – year captain of year eight," the Sheikh continued, smiling. "What do you have to say?"

Yusif paused for a moment. His heart was pounding at the prospect of such a position. One part of him wanted to draw back – perhaps he should settle in a bit longer at the school? Another part thought back to his parents, and how proud they would be to hear the news. No, he would clear his mind, and do what would be best for his *deen*.

Yusif took a deep breath in, and spoke.

"Sheikh Ansari, it is a great honour for me to be offered this position, and I would be prepared to accept it, *inshallah!*"

The decision was heartily welcomed by everyone in the room. As Yusif moved to leave, Abdul Kadir smiled warmly, raising his arm to his chest and nodding his head slightly forward, as if to reassure Yusif that he had made the right decision. Yusif remembered back to the discussion that the pair had had outside the dorms. Time had certainly flown by since then!

Yusif's decision was equally well received by the other boys. Reda and Daud were elated. Even Warsoma who himself had been nominated, was quick to congratulate his friend. In fact, Yusif had made such a good impression upon his fellow pupils, that there was not a single boy in Ibn Kathir House to raise a serious objection to his nomination for the role of year captain.

A week later, it was the last day of term. For the last time that year, the boys of year seven congregated with the rest of the school in the main prayer hall. This was a very special day and every student was excited. Not only was it the end of the academic year, with the prospect of a fun-filled summer holiday, but it was also the day they would finally discover who the year captains for each year group would be.

In all, three boys from Ibn Kathir house had been nominated for year eight. They were Warsoma, Azmi and Yusif himself. The gathered audience waited patiently for the result.

In the days that had followed the announcement of the winning house, candidates had been put forward for year captain.

Then there was Speech Day, where all the candidates were expected to give a short presentation, addressing their peers about their reasons for aspiring to be the year captain. For Yusif, it was a terrifying prospect, but he had made his best efforts to explain how he would fulfil his duties, if he were appointed.

Shortly after this, the boys of the year had cast their votes for their preferred candidates from the three nominees. The votes were counted and considered by Sheikh Ansari and the housemasters, with whom the final decision lay.

Yusif looked at his co-nominees Warsoma and Azmi. He would have been happy to step down to either one of them. He loved both of them as his Muslim brothers and felt that either of them would have made excellent year captains.

Sheikh Ansari stood at the front of the hall, holding his teaching staff by his side. Raising his right hand, he gave an indication to the room to settle down, and then he addressed the congregation. His speech contained various messages about the year gone by, plans for the forthcoming year, and advice about keeping up studies during the holidays. Eventually he turned his attention to the matter of the year captains.

He began with year seven, reading out the names of the three candidates. He asked them to join him at the front of the room. Yusif, Warsoma and Azmi rose up and nervously made their way forward. They stood beside each other, facing the audience, their hearts fluttering with nerves. Warsoma's stomach was churning.

"I would like to start by congratulating the three of you," said Sheikh Ansari. "It is a testament to your good standing in the school that you have been chosen by your peers to represent them. After taking into account the votes, and considering the matter very carefully, the housemasters, the head boy and I, have come to a decision. The year captain for the forthcoming year will be...*Yusif Abdur-Raheem!*"

With this announcement, the prayer hall filled with gasps and cheers from the boys of year seven. Warsoma and Azmi both stepped forward to shake Yusif's hand and embrace him. Yusif was quite shocked by the result, but smiled nonetheless. Sheikh Ansari was quick to silence the celebrations, reminding everyone that he still had another five year captains to reveal and, of course, the new head boy!

It was almost an hour later by the time the boys had arrived in the Great Hall to celebrate.

Reda and Daud were overjoyed at the news of Yusif's appointment. Yusif himself was surrounded by his year group, who were at the same time congratulating him and commiserating with Warsoma and Azmi. Warsoma, of course, was secretly relieved, his stomach now very much more settled. The last time he had felt this bad was at the thought of climbing in the Brecon Beacons last year. Until today, he had thought nothing could ever beat that!

Khalid made his way through the crowd of boys, and tapped Yusif on the shoulder.

"I hoped you would win. You are a worthy choice!" said Khalid, offering his hand forward. Yusif smiled, took it warmly with both hands and shook it.

"I mean it..." continued Khalid. "You truly deserved to win and I'm happy for you! I'm only sorry for all the trouble I caused."

"It's alright," said Yusif. "No one's perfect, Khalid. Anyone can make a mistake!"

"No I was *stupid*," insisted Khalid. "I couldn't understand why everyone liked you and I became jealous, *astaghfirullah*. When I was new in the school, I was scared. I was worried I wouldn't make any friends. I thought if I impressed people and showed how clever I was, then they would like me. But I was wrong – they didn't seem to like me. I wanted to be year captain for all the wrong reasons, but you never did *alhamdulillah*! I hope you will be able to forgive me."

"Of course I forgive you Khalid," said Yusif, feeling a little sorry for him. "And perhaps you will win year captain next time, *inshallah!*"

Khalid shrugged his shoulders. "Maybe, if Allah wills!" he said. At this, Yusif suddenly had a thought.

"Sheikh Ansari said that I would need representatives from the other houses to help me next year," said Yusif.

"He said I could choose from amongst the nomination candidates. You were nominated by Ibn Majah House. I was wondering, would you like to represent them and help me?" asked Yusif.

Khalid's mouth fell wide open in amazement.

"*Really* – are you sure you want me to help?" he asked.

Yusif nodded his head. "I think you have a lot of good ideas," he said. "I especially liked your suggestion of a *tajweed* club. I think we could make a good team!"

Khalid smiled and humbly accepted Yusif's offer. After that, the gathered boys wished each other a happy break, exchanging handshakes, hugs and addresses. Yusif invited Khalid to visit him over the holidays. Khalid's spirits rose with this kind gesture, and the pair parted company very cheerfully.

Abdul Kadir was the next in line to congratulate Yusif.

"*Mabrook!* I'm very proud of you *akhi*," he said. "I'm confident you'll do a great job, *inshallah*. I only wish I could have had the opportunity to work with you on the student council. But I've asked the new head boy to keep a look out for you."

Yusif had forgotten that Abdul Kadir would be leaving at the end of the year. Abdul Kadir noticed a sudden disappointment in Yusif's eyes.

"Don't look so worried! Ismail is a very good brother. I think you will like him and he will help you, *akhi*. Although I must say, he's more likely to need *your* help than you'll need his."

Yusif smiled, much relieved by his words. He knew that he was really going to miss Abdul Kadir, who was going on to medical school in London after the summer.

They bade farewell to each other. Abdul Kadir promised to pay a return visit to the school the next year.

"I can't believe it's finally the holidays," said Daud.

"Are you going abroad to visit your parents?" asked Yusif.

"Yes, with my grandfather. It's a good thing too. I have a lot to discuss with him on the flight about the primordial soup theory! What are you doing?"

"I'm not sure yet!" shrugged Yusif. "How about you three?" asked Yusif turning to look at Reda, Warsoma and Azmi.

"Jordan again!" said Reda excitedly.

"I'm going home to Kuala Lumpur!" replied Azmi.

"Well that just leaves me and Warsoma to meet up over the holidays, since everyone else is abandoning us and leaving the country!" said Yusif, throwing his arms up in the air.

The boys laughed. They bade their farewells and

parted company.

Yusif found his parents talking to Ustad Ibrahim in the Great Hall. The memory of the tunnel fiasco came flooding back to him. What on earth were his parents going to say? He approached them with much trepidation.

Yusif's mother was the first to spot him. She moved away from her husband and Ustad Ibrahim, and headed straight for her son. She hugged him so hard that he could barely breathe against her hijab.

"Ammi – you're choking me!"

"Nonsense – Ooh, I missed you! Well how was your first year?" she asked anxiously. It was something she had avoided asking at his first visit home. Yusif looked at her for a moment, exaggerating his indecisiveness before blurting out excitedly, "*Alhamdulillah*, it was just great!" he laughed.

"I think I was scared at the thought of such a big change in my life. But I've learned a lot since I've been away. I'm not so scared of change anymore! Change can be good," admitted Yusif.

"Well, I'm glad you said that because there's more change to come!" exclaimed Ammi. Yusif raised a puzzled eyebrow at the remark. What could she be referring to?

"She'll be here soon!" she said. In that moment he realised Ammi was talking about the baby and remembered that he was finally going to be a brother!

"Is it a girl?" asked Yusif excitedly.

"Well only Allah knows for certain! But either way you're going to have to be very responsible.

It's a big job being the big brother, a bit like being year captain!" laughed Ammi. Yusif blushed as he realised that his mother already knew about his election to the position.

"Ustad Ibrahim tells us you've done really well this year. Fancy being chosen as year captain in your first year at the school! And we heard that you found some ancient coins – I'm looking forward to seeing them!"

"Ah! I'm afraid we had to hand them over to the local authorities," said Ustad Ibrahim, overhearing Ammi, as he and Abu joined them.

"But Yusif does have plenty of photographs," said Ustad Ibrahim to the proud parents. He looked at Yusif warmly.

"Well, Yusif, I hope you found your stay here enjoyable. We had a few hiccups, but otherwise a very good year!" He smiled reassuringly at Yusif.

He had briefed Yusif's parents earlier about the tunnels, and they had taken it quite well after assurances from Ustad Ibrahim that no harm had befallen Yusif or anyone else. Ustad Ibrahim finally parted company with the family, wishing them a good summer break.

"Are you ready to go home, son?" asked Abu.

Yusif grinned. He turned to look back round at the old school building for a moment. He remembered the first time that he had laid eyes upon it a year ago, and how nervous he had been about coming there. Then it had been an almost daunting sight, with its tall grey walls and seemingly endless maze-like corridors.

But now, things were different. The old walls were crawling with wisteria vines, and all manner of summer shrubs and flowers decorated the borders around the building. The sun shone brightly above, illuminating the place with vibrant shades of red, purple and yellow. Never expecting that he would grow to like the place so much, Yusif turned back towards his father.

"Yes, I'm ready, Abu..." he said grinning. "Let's go."

The House of Abu Hanifa

The House of Abu Hanifa is named after one of the four 'Great Imams', Nu'man ibn Thabit ibn Zuta ibn Mahan, who is better known by his *kunya* or nickname, of Imam Abu Hanifa. He was born in 80 AH in Iraq where he lived, grew up and studied.

Imam Abu Hanifa was renowned for his exceptional intellect and skills in debate, scrupulousness, personal integrity and for his bravery in the face of oppression before an unjust ruler. During his lifetime he was known to have met companions of the Prophet (peace be upon him), and for this reason he is counted amongst the *tabi'un* - those who are considered to be from the second generation of Muslims.

He was most famous for being a scholar of *fiqh*, the science of Islamic jurisprudence. This branch of knowledge is concerned with the rules and laws that Muslims have been commanded by Allah (all praise be to Him) to follow. These rules are derived from the Noble Qur'an and the *sunnah* of the Prophet (peace be upon him), and give guidance on every aspect of the lives of the Muslims, both as individuals and as a collective society.

Imam Abu Hanifa was also a master of numerous other Islamic disciplines, and was noted for his profound knowledge of *aqeeda*, the detailed elaboration of the Islamic beliefs.

The legacy of his juristic studies and knowledge has been referred to by Muslims over a period that spans more than twelve centuries. His *madhab*, or school of Islamic law was particularly used during the Abbasid and Ottoman Caliphates, and also during the Mughal reign in India. Imam Abu Hanifa's legacy is his teachings of the Sacred Knowledge, which continue to be widely followed by Muslims all over the world today.

Imam Abu Hanifa (80AH-150AH)

The House of
Ibn Majah

The House of Ibn Majah is named after Abu
Abdallah Muhammad ibn Yazid ibn Majah al-Rabi
al-Qazwini, otherwise referred to as Ibn Majah. He
was a scholar of *hadith*, which are the sayings of the
Prophet Muhammad (peace be upon him). He was
born in the year 209 AH in the town of Qazwin, not
far from today's Tehran. Ibn Majah studied from
a great number of teachers and travelled widely in
his quest to acquire knowledge through many different
lands including Basra, Baghdad, Syria, Cairo and
the Hijaz.

As the Muslim frontiers expanded during the early years of Islamic history, the *sahaba* (may Allah be pleased with them) and their successors travelled far and wide with the aim of teaching the religion to those who embraced Islam. Consequently, knowledge of Islam became widely dispersed. Since then, travelling in the search for knowledge has been undertaken by Muslims. It is a noble act for those whose aim is to understand the message of Islam.

The speech and actions of the Prophet Muhammad are part of the revelation from Allah (all praise be to Him). The science of *hadith* is a precise subject that is aimed at checking and preserving the prophetic guidance in its original form. This was done by documenting the chains of narrators of *hadith*, and checking the reliability of each narrator in the chain. *Hadith* scholars like Ibn Majah, would go to considerable lengths to seek out or verify new *hadiths*, often travelling great distances for the purpose.

His mastery of the knowledge of the Prophetic narrations enabled him to author his 'Sunnan Ibn Majah', one of the six principle *hadith* collections of Sunni Islam.

The age of Imam Ibn Majah was characterised with a zeal for travelling in the pursuit of knowledge and it was through such journeys that generations of Muslims after have benefited. Until this day, many have been inspired by the likes of this great scholar, to follow in the same footsteps and with the same spirit of learning.

Ibn Majah (209AH-273AH)

The House of
Ibn Kathir

The House of Ibn Kathir is named after Imad
Ad-Din Ismail ibn Umar ibn Kathir Al-Quraishi
Al-Busrawi, otherwise known as Imam Ibn Kathir.
He was born in the year 701 AH in the city of Busra.
He was known for his remarkable memory, clear and
profound understanding of the Qur'an, and superior
grasp of the Arabic language.

Imam Ibn Kathir is best remembered for his four
volume Tafsir of Al-Qur'an – a commentary and
explanation of the divine revelation. It is a book that
has been taught and relied upon by generations of

Islamic scholars and their students.

The science of *tafsir* is concerned with the elaboration and explanation of the meanings of the verses of the Qur'an. Consideration is given to the deeper Arabic meanings of the words and phrases mentioned in the divine speech. Among many other factors, the circumstances in which the *ayats* were revealed to the Prophet (peace be upon him) are noted, as well as the related Prophetic sayings, both of which have an impact on how the verses are interpreted.

Although the Qur'an was revealed 1400 years ago, the guidance it contains can be applied in all times and places. The reason for this is that the Qur'anic rules address the principles by which people live. So wherever people are in the world, and whatever their level of technological advancement, the principles of conduct laid down in the Qur'an can be followed.

Imam Ibn Kathir had many other accomplishments. He was a hadith master, memorizing a large number of the sayings of the Prophet (peace be upon him). He became a leading scholar of the Shafi'i *madhab*, and a historian who authored works in both of these fields.

Ibn Kathir (701AH-774 AH)

The House of Ibn Ajeroom

The House of Ibn Ajeroom is named after Abu 'Abdillah Muhammad ibn Muhammad ibn Daawud as-Sanhaajee, who was known as Ibn Aajeroom. He was an Islamic jurist, a mathematician, an expert in the field of Arabic grammar and syntax and he had vast knowledge of other sciences including *tajweed*.

He was born in the year 672 AH in Fez, Morocco. He grew up and studied there for some time until he desired to perform pilgrimage to Makkah. During his journey he passed through Cairo and remained there for a while to study under the direction of the

Andalusian grammarian Abu Hayan Muhammad ibn Yusuf al-Granati.

During his stay in Makkah he authored his most famous work 'the Ajroomiya', which became the standard text for students of Arabic grammar. After he left Makkah he returned to Fez where he remained to teach Arabic grammar and the Qur'an in the Mosque of the Andalusian Quarter, until he died.

There has been a long history of the preservation of the Arabic language in its purest form. The second Caliph Umar (may Allah be pleased with him) said, 'Learn Arabic for it is part of your religion'. Later, the fourth Caliph Ali (may Allah be pleased with him), noticed in the speech of some of the Arabs a slight change in their articulation. He ordered for the grammar rules of Arabic to be recorded in a standardised form, for he realised that preservation of the Arabic language was vital for the preservation of Islam itself.

The Arabic language united Muslims, whether Arab or non-Arab, all over the Islamic lands and civilisation flourished under its wing. Whatever their race, colour or place of origin, citizens identified themselves with this civilisation and it was the richness and flexibility of the Arabic language that bound them to it. The Qur'an is the word of Allah (all praise be to Him); a direct message from Allah to His creation and Allah chose the Arabic language as the language of this message.

Ibn Ajeroom (672AH-723AH)

Glossary of Arabic Terms

Adhan: The call to prayer, which is called loudly from every mosque at the time of each prayer.

Akhi: Brother.

Akhirah: The hereafter, which is after the life of this world.

Al-Amin: The Trustworthy one; it is a name by which the Holy Prophet Muhammad (may peace and blessings be upon him) was known before he became a prophet.

Al-baqarah: The second chapter of the Holy Qur'an, 'the heifer'. It is the longest chapter in the Holy Qur'an.

Al-fatihah: the first chapter of the Holy Qur'an, 'the opening'. It is recited in every prayer.

Al-thawr: The name of the cave in which the Holy Prophet Muhammad (may peace and blessings be upon him) and his companion Abu Bakr (may Allah be pleased with him), sought refuge when they were being pursued by the Quraysh at the time of their emigration from Makkah.

Alhamdulillah: 'All praise is to Allah'.

Asr: the mid-afternoon prayer.

Assalaamu alaikum wa rahmatullahi wa barakatuhu: 'May peace be upon you, and the mercy and the blessings of Allah'.

Astaghfirullah: 'Oh, Allah forgive me'.

Ayat al-kursi: 'The verse of the throne', which is the 255th verse of surah al-baqarah. It is often recited by Muslims to seek the protection of Allah (all praise be to Him).

Barakah: Blessings.

Basmala: To say 'bismillah'.

Bismillah: 'In the name of Allah'.

Caliph: Leader of the Muslims. They are the successors to the Prophet Muhammad (peace be upon him) in ruling over the people. The first four of them were known as the 'Rightly Guided Caliphs', and they were Abu Bakr, Umar, Uthman and Ali (may Allah be pleased with them all).

Deen: Religion, or 'way of life'.

Dhikr: Remembrance of Allah (all praise be to Him).

Dhuhr: The afternoon prayer.

Dua: Supplication, to ask Allah (all praise be to Him) for something.

Fajr: The morning prayer.

Fez: A style of hat originating from a city in Morocco.

Fiqh: Islamic rules.

Foo yoo: An expression of surprise used by many people from Malaysia.

Hadeeth: A saying of the Holy Prophet Muhammad (may peace and blessings be upon him).

Hafiz: A person who has memorised the entire Qur'an.

Halal: An action or a thing that is lawful according to the rules of Islam. Food that is permitted for Muslims to eat.

Haram: An action or a thing that is unlawful according to the rules of Islam.

Hari raya: The name used by people from Malaysia to refer to 'Eid' - a day of celebration for Muslims.

Hijrah: The emigration of the Holy Prophet Muhammad (may peace and blessings be upon him) from Makkah to Medina.

Iman: 'Faith', or the belief of a Muslim.

Inshallah: 'If Allah wills'. A Muslim should say this when they intend to do something, or if they have hope that something will happen.

Iqamah: The call to start the prayer. It is given after the adhan, immediately before the beginning of any of the five daily prayers.

Isha: The night prayer.

Isti'adha: To seek refuge in Allah (all praise be to Him) from the accursed shaitan (the devil).

Istikharah: A prayer where one seeks guidance from Allah (all praise be to Him) over a matter in which one needs to make a decision.

Itr: Scented oil or perfume.

Jalabiya: A long garment, usually worn by men in the Arabic world.

Jama'ah: When a prayer is made in congregation.

Jazakallah khairan: 'May Allah reward you well'.

Jumah: The weekly congregational prayer, which is held every Friday. It is obligatory for all Muslim males to attend.

Khalas: A word used to mean 'that is the end of the matter'.

Khutbah: A religious speech or sermon, given by the imam before the jumah prayer.

Mabrook: 'Congratulations'.

Maghrib: The sunset prayer.

Mashallah: 'By the grace of Allah'.

Mihrab: The niche in the wall of the mosque, indicating the direction of prayer.

Minbar: A raised pulpit in the mosque from where the imam delivers the Friday sermon.

Mu'adhin: The person who makes the call to prayer.

Nam: 'Yes'.

Rakat: Cycles of prayer (plural), rakah (singular).

Sajadah: A carpet or prayer mat.

Salah: The prayer.

Salams: The greetings offered between Muslims.

Silat: A type of martial art, originating from south east Asia.

Souk: The market.

Subhanallah: 'Glory be to Allah'.

Sunnah: The practice of the Holy Prophet Muhammad (may peace and blessings be upon him).

Surah: A chapter of the Holy Qur'an.

Surah yasin: The 36th chapter of the Holy Qur'an.

Tafseer: A commentary about the meanings of the Holy Qur'an.

Tajweed: The correct manner of recitation of the Holy Qur'an, following specific rules. This helps Muslims to recite the Qur'an in the precise manner that it was recited by the Prophet Muhammad (peace be upon him).

Takbir: To say 'Allah is the Greatest'.

Taqwa: Piety, or the fear of Allah (all praise be to Him).

Tasleem: The final salam which is said at the end of each prayer.

Topee: A style of hat worn by male Muslims.

Umrah: The lesser pilgrimage to Makkah.

Wudu: Ablution; the washing of parts of the body to obtain ritual purity before prayer or touching of the Holy Qur'an. It involves washing the face and hands, wiping over the head and washing the feet.

Ya Allah: 'Oh Allah!'.

Ya habib: 'Oh my beloved friend!'.

Ziyarah: A trip or journey.

Qur'anic References

Page 139, Ref : Surah 24:45
Page 141, Ref : Surah 45:3-5